GU

Stephen Baxter was born in Liverpool, and attended Cambridge University. Since then he has worked in engineering, teaching and computing. He has had several adult science-fiction novels published by HarperCollins.

Other titles in the
THE WEB series

DREAMCASTLE

UNTOUCHABLE

SPIDERBITE

LIGHTSTORM

SORCERESS

SERIES EDITOR
Simon Spanton

For more information about the books, compe-
titions and activities, check out our website:
http://www.orionbooks.co.uk/web

THE WEB
GULLIVERZONE

◆

STEPHEN BAXTER

Orion Children's Books
and

Dolphin Paperbacks

For
James, Thomas and William Baxter,
Jessica Bourg,
Kay and Max Sharpington
Rebecca and Eleanor Cousins
Amy, James and Mary Oliver

First published in Great Britain in 1997
as an Orion hardback
and a Dolphin paperback
by Orion Children's Books
a division of the Orion Publishing Group Ltd
Orion House
5 Upper St Martin's Lane
London WC2H 9EA

Second impression 1998

A catalogue record for this book is available
from the British Library

Typeset at The Spartan Press Ltd,
Lymington, Hants
Printed in Great Britain by
Clays Ltd, St Ives plc

ISBN 1 85881 475 8 (hb)
ISBN 1 85881 423 5 (pb)

CONTENTS

CHAPTER ONE

WEBSUITS

I set my bedroom to wake me early.

It was World Peace Day. And today I was going to spin into the Web and access GulliverZone.

Maybe you spun in too. Maybe we even met. Everybody seemed to be there!

I thought my biggest problem was going to be having the most unpopular girl at school *and* my dumb little brother, tagging along with me.

How wrong can you be!

I'd never have gone into GulliverZone – in fact I think I'd have stayed in bed that morning – if I'd known how close I would come to never getting out again . . .

The bedroom chimed softly.

'Good morning, Sarah,' it said.

I groaned and turned over. 'Metaphor. My name is Metaphor.'

'I'm not programmed to use aliases,' the bedroom said primly.

'Of course you are.' It was dark outside. 'What time is it?'

'Six a.m.'

'*Six!* What is it, Christmas Day?'

'No, Sarah. It is Sunday, February 7, 2027—'

'Sunday? Well, you can shut yourself off and let me sleep.'

'. . . and it's World Peace Day.'

Oh, wow. *Now* I remembered.

I sat up in bed and rubbed my eyes. 'Give me the news.'

'Which channel?'

'BBC 34.'

One whole side of my bedroom lit up with images.

There was a picture of a big celebration going on in a stadium in Pusan, in South Korea: thousands of people, fireworks, singers and dancers, and a platform full of world leaders. I could see our Prime Minister, Ravi Sivarajan, along with King William, President Samuel Jackson of the US, and Boris Becker, Chancellor of United Europe. They were listening to a poem by the Poet Laureate, Damon Albarn.

I told the bedroom to flick around. This was the twentieth World Peace Day, so there were celebrations *everywhere*.

At the Vatican, the Pope was blessing the crowds, his shining black face split by smiles. In Las Vegas, the Robot Beatles were performing *Sergeant Pepper*. Wembley was staging a laser-show hologram match between the England Euro 96 soccer team and the 2026 World Cup winners, Kenya. The real Euro 96 team had been brought out of retirement to see the match, and sat in the stand like a row of grey old soldiers. I imagined Philip complaining about that. *Why don't they make footballers like they used to in this country? It's all money now. Look at Paul Gascoigne. There was a player for you . . .*

(Philip's my dad, by the way. He lets me call him Philip. I let him call me Metaphor.)

On the frozen Thames there was a huge bonfire and a skating gala. In Germany, one of the five-hundred-metre balls of carbon dioxide pollution they froze out of the air had been sculpted into the shape of a huge dove. (Cor-*ny*.) Over the North Pole, the big airship they put up to fix the ozone layer had WORLD PEACE scrolling its mile-wide belly. Pusan was the centre of the celebrations, of course. That was where the North Koreans dropped their atomic bomb in 2007, the event that started the whole World Peace movement in the first place. And at Cape Canaveral, one of the Mars astronauts was waving as he got on board the Space Shuttle *Eagle* . . .

'Off,' I said. The wall blanked out.

So; all that stuff going on, all over the world.

Big deal! I wasn't interested in any of it.

Because today, GulliverZone – the best theme park in the Web – was going to be *free* . . .

I went to the bathroom and washed.

Philip had the mirror tuned to the Snow White option as usual, but I turned that off. I like to know what I *look* like, not what I'd *prefer* to look like. Maybe when you get to Philip's advanced age the truth is just too awful to bear.

I got dressed quickly and ran downstairs. I would have a quick breakfast and spin in, I decided, before Philip had a chance to lumber me with—

George.

The little egg was already sitting at the breakfast table. His favourite animatronic *Action Man* was frisbeeing edible pogs into his mouth. He is *such* a one-mip kid.

Personally, I eat nothing but adult breakfasts. I poured myself a huge bowl of cola-flavoured cereal.

I had to clear last night's empty TFO (Tennessee Fried Ostrich) boxes off the table. And before I ate I put out a bowl of food for our cat, Gazza. When he smelled the food he came in through the catflap, shook snow off his orange fur, and tucked in.

I raised my first mouthful, and slowed.

The egg was grinning at me. I had the horrible feeling he was planning something.

'Good morning, *George*,' I said.

That wiped the grin off his face. 'Byte!' he said. 'Call me Byte.'

'You're too young to have an alias.'

'I'm not too young to spin into the Web.'

I froze. I even stopped ladling cola pops into my mouth.

So that was it. I had an awful feeling, a deep and dark dread, in the pit of my stomach .

I said, 'You are *not* spinning in with me today.'

'Oh yes I am,' he said, and he got off his chair and started jumping up and down. He knows I hate that. 'Dad says I can. GulliverZone. GulliverZone. I'm going to GulliverZone.'

'You little egg! Stop jumping! I'm not taking you to GulliverZone!'

He stopped jumping and adopted his most sickening angelic grin. 'Hello, Dad,' he said.

Behind me, Philip had come into the kitchen. His hair was all over the place, and he was wearing a horrible sweatshirt, so old it showed Noel Gallagher *before* he was knighted. As usual, he fell for George's ploy. He ruffled the kid's hair.

It drove me crazy. Just the day before, George had used the same tactics to raise his pocket money to a hundred Euros a week. I was *ten* before I got a hundred – two years older than George. Even *now* I'm only on a thousand a week.

Philip yawned and went to the coffee tap. 'What's Sallibugs shouting at you about?'

I rose to my full height. I have not responded to Sallibugs since I was six years old.

'She says I can't go to GulliverZone,' whined George.

Philip frowned at me. It was his I'm-disappointed-in-you look. I hate it when he does that. 'Is this true?'

I tried not to whine. 'But today's World Peace Day!'

'So stop fighting with your brother,' Philip said, and George started jumping up and down again.

'He'll ruin it.'

'How can one small boy ruin a worldwide celebration?'

'It's just not fair.'

'I know, Metaphor. Lots of things aren't fair.' He gave me his Sarah-we're-adults-together look. I hate that one even more. Because it means I definitely can't get away with it.

I was stuck with the kid. What was worse, I was going to have to spend my whole time showing the little one-mip what to do. I knew he'd only ever used gag before to spin into the Web.

Philip tuned the toaster to his me-paper. He got a status update from Tilbury – the place he works, the Tilbury Desalination Plant – and started reading earnestly.

The conversation, it seemed, was over.

I ate my cola pops in black depression.

We keep our Websuits in the spare bedroom.

My suit was lying on the floor where I'd left it last night. It looked like a diver's wet suit made out of bright orange material, with its built-on head covering, gloves and boots. There were several fine connectors sprouting from the suit's neck. They joined up to a big thick cable that led to a data socket in the wall.

In there as well was Philip's big Websuit – it looked like a 1990s ski jump outfit, *so* unfashionable – and my old kid-sized suit I had grown out of. In the corner there was the gag, the baby gloves-and-glasses kit George had used to spin into the Web up to now.

It was all new to George. He was running around the room like the kid he was. But I knew I had a moment of revenge coming up.

I held up my old little girl's Websuit. 'Here you are, George. Hop in.'

He stopped running. 'I can't wear *that*.'

'Oh? What's wrong, is it the pink colour? The ballerina skirt?'

'No,' he whispered. '*You've* been in it. *Ugh*.'

'Now, come along, George,' Philip said. I hadn't seen him enter the room. 'Be sensible. You know you'll have to wait until your birthday for your own suit. Be a good boy now, and do what your big sister says.'

'I'd rather *die*,' he said.

'If you'd rather not go—'

'I'll put it on,' he said miserably. He opened up the suit by the big zipper down the front and started to climb in.

I started to pull my own suit on. You know what that's like. The suits are one-piece and a tight fit. You really have to wriggle to get into them.

They're supposed to be tight, of course. Everything you feel, touch, see, hear when you're in Webtown comes via your Websuit; through the places it touches your skin, the little screens over your eyes, and so on.

Even so, it was a struggle.

'I think my suit's getting a little tight,' I said to Philip.

'Already? You're growing too fast.'

'Tell me about it,' I said gloomily. I only wished I could grow faster. I was tired of being the smallest kid in the class. If you're short, nobody takes you *seriously*.

'Listen, Metaphor. I have to go in to work.'

I frowned. This was always happening. 'But it's World Peace Day. And it's *Sunday*. Do you have to?'

He sighed and rubbed his tired face. 'You know I do. Otherwise, half of London will be drinking salty sea water by tea time.'

'Does this mean we can't spin in?'

'No.' He looked at me seriously. 'But you're in charge, Metaphor. Take care of Byte.'

'I know how I'd like to take care of him.'

'I'm not kidding,' he said gravely. 'Don't let him get Websick. Three hours maximum, then out.'

'You can trust me, Philip.'

He nodded. He gave me one of his I-know-I-can looks. That one, I don't mind.

'Oh. I nearly forgot,' he said. 'There's something else.'

'What?'

He turned to the door. 'Come on in.'

In walked Meg Toffler, a girl from my class at school. Also known as the Wire. She had a thin, strained-looking face, and she smiled at me in her feeble way. 'Hello, Sarah.'

'Hello.' I glared at Philip and hissed so she couldn't hear. 'What is *she* doing here?'

He looked even more tired. 'You know her father works at Tilbury with me. He just called. He has to work today too. I said she could come in with you today. She can use my suit—'

'You did *what*?'

'Now, Sarah—'

'Meg Toffler is a *wipeout*. And I should know.'

That was true. She seemed to be in every one of my classes at school: Rocket Science, Life Creation, even the boring stuff like Bungee Jumping. I probably knew her as well as anyone else.

And I needed a *holiday*.

Philip got a little angry. 'I don't know what you're complaining about. You only have to go to school two days a week. Now, in my day—'

'Oh, *Philip*.'

'Look, maybe Meg is unhappy right now. But her mother and father are splitting up. Remember how you were when Mum died?' He touched my shoulder. 'Maybe you were a bit of a wimp then too.'

'Wipeout. The word is wipeout.'

'Whatever. Anyway—'

'All right. She can come. She'd just better not start complaining, that's all.'

'That's my girl,' he said.

My day was going from bad to worse. First my basement-level brother, and now the Wire.

Of course if I'd known how bad it was going to get later, I wouldn't have complained . . .

The Wire climbed into Philip's suit. Philip checked over George, while I laughed at the big baby in the ballerina skirt.

'The main thing you need to know,' Philip told George, 'is how to scuttle.'

'Scuttle?'

'If you want to spin out in a hurry. Just press this button on the control panel on your wrist.' Philip showed him. 'See? Then you'll be straight back out here, in Realworld.'

George practised a couple of times.

Philip prepared to leave. 'I don't know about this Web stuff. I remember the good old days when the whole family would gather round the glow of the TV together—'

'And you could buy a newspaper for five Euros,' I said. 'We know the story, Philip.'

He grinned. 'Have fun. Do what the Spiders tell you. Don't go on to supertime. Watch out for the bad people. Especially these stories I hear about someone called the Sorceress. Don't take the—'

It was the standard 'don't' lecture. To close him out, I pulled my mask closed over my face and zipped it up. The inside of the suit was warm, a little moist. The spin programs took a moment to kick in. I waited in the dark. I could hear that pest George giggling.

The Sorceress. Talk about children's stories. Everyone knew there was no bad lady living in the Web called the

Sorceress. It was all playground stuff, spread by little kids. And—

Suddenly, without warning, there was blue sky all around me.

CHAPTER TWO

WEBTOWN

I learned in Industrial Archaeology that they had something like the Web even when Philip was a boy, in the 1990s. Amazing. I hadn't even known they had *computers* back then!

There was something called *the Internet*, lots of computers around the world connected in a network by telephone lines. They had *holograms*, free-standing, three-dimensional images. And they even had *Virtual Reality*, which was a bit like spinning into the Web, but . . . well, a lot clunkier. Like comparing a jet fighter with a skateboard.

When you spin into the Web you feel as if you've entered another world. You haven't. You haven't even left your house. It's all made up by networks of computers around the world.

We learned all this at school. I found it really interesting to learn how they build the Webware – the Web software, the instructions for the computers. Maybe I'll be a Webware designer when I get older. If I don't pass the exam to go to the Moon colony, that is.

So I understood how the Web works. But I wasn't about to tell George – oh, all right, *Byte* – any of that.

You know what it's like to enter Webtown's first level. One second we were lying on our backs in our familiar spare room. The next – we were there, suddenly standing up, in the middle of a flat golden plain, like a wheat field, with Building Blocks scattered over it like toys dropped by giant children.

Byte, finding himself standing up like that, lost his balance. He stumbled forward and fell on his belly. He screamed like a baby. It made me feel a lot better.

Even the Wire was laughing. 'It isn't real, silly,' she said. 'That's the whole point. It looks and sounds real, but it isn't. Look.' And she flapped her arms and did a backwards somersault. 'These aren't even our bodies. We look like ourselves – we're even wearing our own clothes. But these bodies are *avatars*. Like electronic puppets, inside the Web. In here, you can't get hurt,' she said. 'Here, you don't even have to wear your skin cream and hat when you go outside in the summer . . .'

And she was right. We were perfectly safe in the Web . . . or so I thought then!

Byte got up, and quietened down. 'Not real?'

'Of course not,' I said.

'I wasn't scared.'

'Oh, you *liar*.'

The Wire said, 'I know that jump is a bit of a shock, but this is the way they let children into the Web. Adults can beam straight to the building block they want to go to, of course.'

Byte nodded seriously.

I snickered. 'He's faking it! He doesn't know what a building block is.'

'Yes, I do.'

'Do not . . .'

And so on, all the way to the nearest building block. Just a day at the office, for a girl and her pesky kid brother.

As we neared the building block we could see we weren't alone on the plain. There was a shadowy suggestion of people around us – like a crowd of ghosts, difficult to make out or count. They can't show you all of the users inside Webtown in person – there are *millions*, it would be impossible – but they like to give the illusion of the crowds present with you if you go somewhere busy. So, the ghosts. It's the kind of thing you pick up as you spend time in Webtown.

Right now, anyhow, I could see we were part of a throng of children, all heading in big thick streams towards the building blocks for Education, Retail, Communication, Library, whatever. The surfaces of the blocks were sparkling, ever-changing. Like big advertizing hoardings for whatever was inside them. Byte's eyes looked like they would bug out of his head.

A lot of kids were heading for Sport. And a *lot* towards Entertainment. That's the place they keep the theme parks.

We joined a river of kids, marching towards the Entertainment Block. One boy worked his way over to us, and when he got close enough he snapped out of the ghost-grey background so we could see him. He was dressed for an interactive game: overalls, hard black body armour that was moulded to his back and chest, boots that laced up to the knees, steel shinpads and a shimmering red cloak. *So* obvious! He smiled at me, a gesture I treated with the contempt it deserved.

Byte looked nervously at the ghosts. 'Won't it be crowded with all these people?'

'Yes,' I said. 'Better scuttle on home, George.'

'No,' said the Wire. 'The Web never gets crowded. It's not real, Byte. It just expands as more people want to use it.'

That's the Wire for you. Truthful, but just *no* sense of humour.

Still, she was right. It you go to a Web theme park *there are never any queues* . . .

We walked into the building block.

It was like dipping into a viscous liquid. I could feel the surface of the block moving over my body, like a rubber band. When my head passed into the building block there was a brief flash of electric blue, and an electronic tone.

The block expanded all around us, just like the Tardis, until skyscrapers filled the plain, all the way to the horizon. That transition happens every day, of course, but even *that* had Byte goggling when I dragged him in after me.

We were standing on a wide boulevard. The sides of the buildings and even the sky were coated with huge ad hoardings. Some of them were three-dimensional – like the one for the *X-Files* ice dance show – even though 3-D ads are supposed to be banned inside the Entertainment block.

And there was a special exhibition, right there in the building block, to celebrate World Peace Day.

For instance, there was a display of what scientists thought life might be like on the planet Bellatrix III, the planet of another star they found recently. And there was a big globe of our world, turning slowly, beamed down from satellites and beefed up by computer graphics. The big superconducting power net was spread all over the globe, shining yellow. The big new irrigation canals in the American midwest were blue threads. Australia was so full of solar farms it seemed to glitter. I could see the new monorail network being built across India in time for next year's Olympics.

The south of Britain was brown and looked dried out – more like the south of Spain used to be, Philip says, back in the stone age when he was a kid, around 1997. And I could see the new energy mats in the Wash, so big they could be seen from space . . .

In the middle of the exhibit there was a Mars astronaut,

lying on his back, working invisible switches. It was the mission commander, Chuck McFarlane. He was wearing a jockey chip today, so we could all follow him as he prepared to take off from Cape Canaveral in a few hours time.

But right now, as you might expect, nobody was paying much attention to Chuck, or any of the serious educational stuff!

It was just chaos in that block. Kids were running *everywhere*. All the theme parks were free today: Cretaceous Park, Apollo 13, the Roald Dahl Adventure Playground, Dreamcastle, Tom Sawyer Country . . . Spiders – Web helpers – were rattling around, trying to control the flow, their cartoon legs whirring like propellers.

Some of the kids were moving a little oddly. Jerkily, like speeded-up characters in a cartoon.

'Wow,' said Byte. 'That looks great.' He started hopping around, waving his arms and legs like Daffy Duck.

I exchanged a glance with the Wire. Time for the responsible big sister bit, I thought.

'Listen, you one-mip. Those kids are on supertime.'

'Supertime?'

'Look, we're all on Webtime here. Everything is faster for us. It makes things brighter, more colourful, noisier. And some people go on to supertime, which is even quicker.'

'More fun!'

'Well, yes.' I admit I had tried supertime myself. 'But it's bad for you. You have to leave the Web earlier, and when you get home you feel dull. Even duller than you normally are. It's called the slows. So if anyone offers you supertime, say no.'

Byte looked disgruntled.

Now, be careful. I know what's good for you. Don't do anything I wouldn't do . . . The worst thing about having a kid brother is that it turns you into your own parents.

That boy in the black gaming suit had landed close by. His cape was rippling over his shoulders, just like Superman's. 'Hi,' he said to me.

I groaned. 'Oh, no. Bad taste *and* an American.'

He laughed. 'I only said one word!'

'What do you want?'

He shrugged, so casually I could feel myself blush under my mask out in Realworld, and I hated him even more. 'Just being friendly. Where are you guys headed? What about the Endangered Park? That's venomous they tell me. They have pandas and manatees there now . . .'

'I hope you're not the type who likes to go hunting dinosaurs,' I said haughtily.

'I certainly am not,' he said, a bit off balance. 'Actually I think I'll go to Dreamcastle. The best game zone in the Web, right? Although I hear that new place, Tracy Island, is pretty wicked.'

I gagged. '*Wicked*? Which 1990s colony are you from, Bellatrix III?'

'No, New England. My name's Surfer. I—'

'We lost Byte,' said the Wire.

'Good,' I snapped.

But of course I had to look for him.

There are times when being the oldest is such a drag. Like, *all* the time.

He hadn't got far. He was standing with his mouth open under a potato-crisp tree.

'Is this real?'

'Yes,' I said seriously. 'Try one.'

He reached up, plucked a crinkly crisp, and put it in his mouth. He looked confused. 'Ugh. I can't taste it.'

Even the Wire laughed. 'Of course not. You can't taste or smell anything in here.'

'Nothing but your socks, anyway,' I said. 'It's just an ad, you one-mip.'

That boy, Surfer, was still hanging around, grinning at me.

Meeting people from all around the world is one of the features of the Web. Right now, for instance, this character Surfer and I were thousands of kilometres apart, in our Websuits, and yet it seemed as if we were side by side.

Usually this is a good thing. It does depend who you meet, though.

'So,' said Surfer. 'What do you say? Maybe I could tag along.'

'Don't you have any friends?'

The Wire actually told me off. 'Metaphor, don't be so rude.'

Surfer laughed. 'Don't worry. It's only because she likes me.'

I started to figure out ways of telling him how wrong he was. Starting with a punch on the nose. It wouldn't hurt in Webtown, but—

Byte was tugging at my hand. 'Let's go. Let's *go*.' He can be such a baby.

I nodded to the Wire. We got hold of Byte's hands, and we started tapping the access code into our wrist controls.

Surfer spread his hands. 'Is this goodbye? Where are you going?'

I took pity on him. 'There's only one place to go today,' I said.

'Where?'

'GulliverZone!'

We finished entering the code.

There was a blue flash and a beep, and the floor disappeared.

. . . And I was sitting on the palm of a gigantic hand!

CHAPTER THREE

GULLIVERZONE

The three of us were sitting on the fleshy thumb joint of the upturned hand. The skin was very soft and warm and looked as if it ought to smell of soap and perfume. The fingers, curling up a little, were like big pieces of furniture.

The hand was steady, so we were in no danger of falling off. But we were, I guessed, about thirty metres off the ground!

Byte was whimpering, the baby. And the Wire was moaning. 'They might have given us some *warning*.'

I was a little rattled too, but I wasn't about to show it. 'Oh, come on. There's always an access metaphor like this. Something in keeping with the theme of the park. The show's started already. Lighten up, you guys.' And to show I wasn't scared, I got on my tummy and crawled to the edge of the hand.

We were suspended above a sunlit landscape. Below us was a little town. At its centre was a palace, surrounded by a shining moat. Further out I could see tree-clad hills, lakes shining like sheets of glass, and what looked like a herd of white horses galloping over the grass.

It was like being in an aeroplane, except in the open. As you'd imagine a magic carpet ride, I suppose.

But I was looking down along an immense body. I could see two tree-trunk legs planted on the ground, swathed in a

skirt the size of a parachute. The legs ended in two giant
feet, and those white horses were jumping the toes like
fences.

Suddenly the hand was lifted up.

The Wire and Byte tumbled over, yelping, and I fell
forward against the rough flesh of the palm.

A huge face hovered over the hand. It must have been
three metres tall. It was monstrous: eyes like blue balloons,
ears like sculptures of flesh, a few loose strands of hair like
ship's cables.

Byte whimpered, 'Is it a balloon?'

It did look a little like those fancy advertising hot-air
balloons you see at fairs sometimes. But I grinned at the
one-mip and said in my scary voice, 'No. *It's real.*'

But even I was startled when the monster face opened its
mouth!

It drew back its lips in a smile, revealing teeth like rows of
white gateposts.

'Hello,' the head said. It was a girl's voice, but it sounded
like remote thunder. 'My name is Glumdalclitch. I'm from
the land of Brobdingnag, here in GulliverZone.'

'Wow,' said Byte. 'You're a *girl*.'

She laughed. It sounded like cannons going off. 'Of
course I'm a girl. In fact I'm nine years old.' She squinted at
him. 'How old are you?'

'Nine.'

I pinched him.

'Next birthday.'

'Well, we're almost the same then,' she said. 'You're so
cute.'

I looked at the Wire, and we exchanged gagging
gestures. Why do people who don't have kid brothers
always think they are cute?

'You're skin's very smooth,' said the egg, and
Glumdalclitch laughed.

I poked him in the back. 'Of course it is. This isn't *real*. If *you* were blown up to thirty metres high, your nose pores would look like craters on the Moon.'

Byte pulled his tongue, looking embarrassed.

'Thank you for choosing to be visitors to GulliverZone,' said Glumdalclitch politely. 'This is the Web's most famous theme park, and it's all based on the great children's story by Jonathan Swift. Did you know the book was written as long ago as 1726, but it's still read widely today?'

The Wire and I glanced at each other. I had a sinking feeling.

'As you know,' Glumdalclitch said, 'everything is free on World Peace Day. Where would you like to start? You can go to Lilliput, the land of the little people. Or come with me to my home, Brobdingnag. Then there is the land of the Houyhnhnms.' I had to look up the spelling before writing that down. She made it sound like a horse whinny. 'The Houyhnhnms are intelligent horses. You can debate philosophy and politics with them. But watch out for the Yahoos, the wild humans . . .'

Byte, the little egg, started jumping up and down. 'Where are the rides? I want to see the rides!'

For once I kind of agreed with him.

This all sounded a little – well – *worthy*. I knew educational groups had put a lot of money into setting up GulliverZone, along with some commercial sponsors like Tennessee Fried Ostrich and Manchester-Newcastle FC. If it was going to be *instructive*, no wonder Philip had been so ready to let us come here.

I was starting to wonder if we should have gone with that kid Surfer to Dreamcastle instead.

I'd never read *Gulliver's Travels*. If it was all so serious, I probably never would. Well, maybe the effects would be good. And—

A huge shadow swept over us, like a cloud. We all yelped and ducked.

The shadow moved on. I looked up. It wasn't a cloud. It was an *island*, a huge elliptical rock floating in the air, with buildings crusted over the upper surface. The bottom was smooth and shining, and I could see people climbing around staircases and balconies carved into the side. Some of them were dangling fishing lines over the edge. They shouted and waved, and Glumdalclitch waved back.

'I almost forgot,' Glumdalclitch said. 'You can go for a ride on our flying island, Laputa.'

Of course we all disagreed about where to go.

The Wire fancied the flying island. Byte just squealed about rides. In the end, as usual, it was up to me.

I stood up straight and faced Glumdalclitch. 'Lilliput,' I said. 'Take us to Lilliput.'

She smiled and bent down. We had to hang on to her fingers, for fear of falling.

Her hand reached the ground. She tipped it, gently, and we rolled off.

I found myself on a lawn of very fine grass. In the middle of it there was a stand of bushes, two or three metres high.

Glumdalclitch straightened up. It was like staring up at Nelson's Column. 'Have a good day,' she boomed. 'If you need anything just ask a spider, or call for me.' And she turned and walked off, every ten-metre stride making the ground shake. 'Remember that. Call me . . .'

'I liked her,' said Byte.

I wouldn't be doing my job if I let *that* one go. 'George has got a girlfriend. George has got a girlfriend—'

He jumped on me and we started to wrestle. We rolled and fetched up against the little stand of bushes.

The Wire followed us, her faced pursed up as usual. 'I don't suppose you've taken time to look at the trees.'

I pushed Byte away, although he kept pummelling my leg. 'What trees? These bushes?'

'They aren't bushes,' she said. 'Look at the leaves.'

I took a closer look. The leaves were very small, like the leaves of watercress, and I could take two or three on my fingertip. But I recognized their shape.

We have a big old oak tree at the bottom of our garden. But the leaves on our tree are usually bigger than the palm of my hand.

The 'bushes' were oak trees, just two metres tall!

'Wow,' I said.

Byte was tugging at my sleeve. 'Let's go to the town,' he said.

'What town?'

He pointed. 'Over there.'

I looked. There *was* a town – perhaps it was the one with the palace we'd seen from the air – but it looked very small and far away. 'I think that might be too far,' I said. 'It looks kilometres away.'

The Wire was moaning. 'I don't know why Glumdalclitch dumped us in the middle of nowhere like this.'

And Byte was nagging. 'Where are the *rides*?'

This was turning, I thought, into a very bad day.

'Let's walk,' I said angrily. 'It can't be that far.' I set off towards the town.

The Wire and Byte followed, grumbling and nagging as was their wont.

Except for the miniature trees, it was like a walk in the country. A wasp buzzed past my head. There were birds singing in the trees. A black cat looked out of a hedgerow at us. It gave us that blank, piercing stare cats do, decided we were no threat, and loped away in search of lunch.

The vegetation here was all miniature. The cat's 'hedgerow' was actually an orchard of tiny apple trees, for instance. But the animals and insects were our scale.

My gloom deepened. Obviously someone had spent a lot of money and mips – computer power – on all these details. The insects and animals – even the cat – were generated within the Zone – they were *phaces*, like the spiders, fake creatures like cartoons that only existed inside the Web.

I wondered if our cat Gazza would enjoy an adventure in a catty Websuit.

Anyway, it was a bad sign. If you find yourself in a theme park where someone has put in a lot of animals and insects and details like that, it usually means they are trying to be *educational*. And have left no money for the rides.

And then, just to cap it all, it started to rain!

It was very realistic – big deal – and I was soon cold and wet and bored. Here I was, slogging across a field in the rain, with kilometres to go to the town . . .

Except it wasn't kilometres.

The town turned out to be just beyond the edge of the field. We only had to walk about a hundred metres.

The town was *miniature* – like a city of dolls' houses. It was so small it had fooled me into thinking it was much farther away.

The rain stopped. We all slowed down and looked at the city.

'Welcome to Mildendo, our metropolis!'

The voice was tiny and came from down by my feet. It was as if an ant had spoken.

I looked down. There was a man standing there, just by

my shoe. He was wearing a leather waistcoat and carrying a bow and arrow.

'My name is Clefven,' he said.

He couldn't have been more than ten centimetres tall!

CHAPTER FOUR

LILLIPUT

Clefven stared up at us. We just goggled back down at him.

'Well?' he said. 'Aren't you going to tell me who you are?'

The Wire looked at me. 'I'm the Wire,' she stammered. 'And this is Byte, and—'

He cupped his hand to his ear. 'I can't hear you. You're too far away! Could you pick me up, please?'

I said, 'Pick you up?'

'Of course.' He held up his arms, like a little kid. 'Don't be shy.'

I bent down and put my hand flat, palm upwards. He got hold of his bow and arrow, braced himself on my little finger, and hopped aboard.

I lifted him up, carefully, with my other hand cupped underneath for fear of dropping him. He smiled up at me, reassuring.

I don't know if you've ever had a small bird stand on your hand. Holding him felt a little like that. His weight was tiny. I could feel the hard heels of his boots, and his miniature fingers where they clasped on to my fingertip.

'Wow,' said Byte, and he leaned close to Clefven. 'He's just like *Action Man*. Only smaller.'

What a one-mip he is.

'Now,' Clefven said. 'Who did you say you were?'

I introduced the three of us again, with me last.

'You'll remember her,' Byte said meanly. 'She's the one with the huge pores on her nose.'

Too late, I remembered how I had teased him before. My spare hand flew to my face.

Clefven laughed. 'Don't be self-conscious. Everything is smoothed over here. Anyway, even if this was real, I'm sure you'd still be just as pretty . . .'

The Wire rolled her eyes to the sky.

'Are you *real*?' Byte asked.

Clefven laughed. 'No. I wish I was. I'm a phace. Do you know what that means? All the little people you'll see here today are phaces too. My job is to be your guide for your visit to Lilliput,' he said. 'Thanks for visiting us. Where would you like to start? Would you like to see the Imperial Court?'

'We want *rides*,' Byte said. 'Where are the rides?'

Clefven smiled. 'We don't really have rides,' he said. 'It isn't that kind of theme park.'

I groaned. I was right. 'Oh, no. It's educational.'

The Wire looked at me. 'Maybe we should just spin out of here and try somewhere else.'

'Well, that would be a shame,' Clefven said.

Byte was tugging at my sleeve. 'No,' he said. 'I want to see more little people.'

I shrugged at the Wire. She shrugged back at me.

So it was that we decided to stay.

Of course if I'd known what was going to befall us, just minutes after that, I'd have got out of there quick!

Clefven guided us towards the centre of Mildendo, their town. He sat on my hand comfortably, cross-legged, and ate a tiny cheese sandwich he pulled out of his pocket. Phaces can eat in the Web, of course, even though visitors can't.

Byte wanted a turn at carrying him, and although

Clefven said it would be OK, I was *not* going to risk the embarrassment of *that*.

Mildendo was surrounded by a wall about a metre high, and quarter of a metre thick. The wall was made of small bricks each the size of a pencil rubber.

When we were over, there was a scratching sound by my leg. I looked down and saw a huge insect – about half a metre long. It had a shiny black shell and it was working its way along the wall. It had tiny little mandibles – jaws – and it was nibbling at the brickwork. There was something vaguely mechanical about its jaws and clattering limbs.

It was like a dog in a space suit.

'Ugh,' said Byte.

I have to admit I felt the same way myself. 'What's that?'

'It's just a *struldbrug*,' said Clefven. 'It does maintenance. Keeping the fabric of GulliverZone repaired, clearing any mess. It's harmless.'

'Is there a lot of litter?' Byte asked.

'No,' I said. 'Of *course* there's no litter. This is Webtown . . .'

None of this was real – it was all generated by computers – but computer software programs do have faults, and develop glitches. There are even *viruses* – rogue programs that can infest Webware and make it 'ill', just like an infection hurting a person.

This struldbrug was actually a bit of the GulliverZone master program which was going around checking the Webware, and repairing the illusion of reality.

The struldbrug looked creepy, though, like a big black beetle with that shiny black shell, and eyes like grains of sand . . .

Clefven had said it was harmless. But I noticed he was hanging on to my finger a little harder than before, and all the time the struldbrug was near, the Lilliputian never took his eyes off it.

Why should Clefven, a phace, be afraid of a maintenance program? Why should a phace be afraid of anything
at all? Phaces were just computer machines. They couldn't
think.

That was the first time I started to wonder if there was
more to GulliverZone than met the eye!

We looked down over Mildendo.

The town was set out as a square, two hundred metres on
each side.

The layout of the town was based on two wide boulevards
– *wide* meaning about a metre across – which were set out
in a cross shape. The Imperial Court, with its palace and
moat, was at the centre where the boulevards met.

The boulevards divided the town into four quarters.
Three of the quarters were clustered with buildings, their
little roofs shining in the sunlight. In the fourth quarter
there was a park with winding paths and a lake with little
sail boats on it. There was a bandstand, but it was shut up.

The heart of the town was the Imperial Court. It was like
a toy castle. It was surrounded by a square moat two metres
wide, with a drawbridge across it. The palace itself was at
the centre of a courtyard, walled off within the moated
area, with buildings and inner walls. On the banks of the
moat there was a crèche, with huge tables and chairs for
normal-sized visitors – adults with their toddlers. I could
see a gaggle of babies lumbering around there now, their
huge heads looming over the little buildings like moons. I
shuddered. *Babies!*

From a distance the palace looked like a miniature
Buckingham Palace, or maybe a White House, with tiny
glittering windows and balconies and railings and flags
everywhere.

'The palace,' said Clefven, 'is the residence of the
Empress Golbasta: supreme ruler of Lilliput, delight and

terror of the universe . . .' He laughed. 'And so on.' It sounded rather a hollow laugh, however.

'We will *definitely* have to go and see that,' I said. 'After we drop off Byte in the crèche.'

That got me a punch in the leg, but since it didn't hurt, it was worth it.

We started to look around the town. There were a few people our size here, mostly children. They stepped like giants over the houses, and bent down and pointed at stuff.

If you've ever been to Legoland, or Bekonscott, or any of those miniature toytowns, you'll have an idea what Mildendo was like.

Except this was *real*.

The Wire pointed. 'Look. There's Surfer.' She looked at me slyly. 'You remember, Metaphor.'

I sniffed.

I looked sideways, though. It *was* Surfer. You couldn't miss that dumb shiny black suit and the Superman cloak. He looked as if he'd made some friends and was having a good time. I could hear him talking about going to Dreamcastle.

Meanwhile, *I* had the egg and the Wire . . .

On cue, Byte started jumping up and down. 'The lake! Let's go see the boats!'

I stopped him. 'You'll step on somebody, you one-mip. Anyhow, we're going to the palace.'

'Oh, don't be so sour,' the Wire told me. 'Let him see the lake. There's plenty of time.'

She had called *me* sour, in front of my kid brother. Now you can see why she was the most unpopular girl at school.

Anyway, I gave in.

We stepped carefully through the streets, heading for the park.

There were little people *everywhere*. They were all ten or

twelve centimetres tall, like dolls come to life. The children were very cute. The people were shopping at the stores that lined the streets, or sweeping out their houses, or tending their tiny, handkerchief-sized gardens. On the main streets, tiny old-fashioned cars puttered up and down.

Everywhere we went, the people waved at us. Clefven leaned over the edge of my hand and hollered down to them.

We reached the quarter with the park. There was a lot of open space here, and we didn't have to tread so carefully as in the town.

Byte whooped, and ran forward towards the lake.

Clefven stood up on my hand. He looked alarmed. 'Slow down!' he called. 'That lake is deeper than it looks . . .'

But Byte couldn't hear his little voice, and by the time I called—

I don't even have to tell you what happened next.

Byte tripped over an oak tree. He fell forward on his belly, slap into the middle of the pond.

He sent up great waves that rippled to the side of the lake. All the Lilliputian sailors started shouting, and waving their fists at Byte. Some of the yachts capsized, and the Lilliputians bobbed about in the water like matchsticks in a bath.

It was just so *typical*.

I ran towards the lake. I was going to give him a piece of my mind. I was so embarrassed I wanted to die.

I noticed there were struldbrugs, dozens of them, scurrying across the park towards the lake. They looked like a pack of dogs, converging on Byte. Lilliputians had to scurry out of their way.

'Get him out,' Clefven said to me.

'Oh, let the little egg take a bath.'

He kicked the ball of my thumb, hard. 'I mean it. Get him out of there. You don't understand.'

I looked into his miniature face. He was serious.

Suddenly, there was a blue flash from the pond.

Byte sank out of sight.

The Wire said, puzzled. 'That looked like the flash you get when you go into a building block. It shouldn't happen *here*. I think something is wrong.'

The struldbrugs were crowding around the pond now, clicking their metallic jaws at each other. Some of them had even jumped in the water, and were swimming around.

Something, I sensed, really was going wrong. And my little brother was in the middle of it.

I could only think of one thing to do.

I ran forward. I closed my hands over Clefven, who was clinging on grimly to my fingers. The Wire called after me, but I ignored her.

I jumped as far as I could, right into the middle of the pond!

I hit the water. It felt wet, but only briefly. It was as if I was falling through a shell of water, into some empty space underneath.

There was a blue flash and a beep.

I fell about two metres. I landed heavily.

I was in a dusty, shed-like space, like the back of a theatre behind the scenery.

I still had Clefven in my hand. I lifted him up. He looked bedraggled and angry.

'Are you all right?' I asked.

'Yes, no thanks to you,' he snapped. 'But you aren't! You shouldn't be here.'

'What do you mean?'

But before he had a chance to answer, I heard a rustling at my feet.

Lilliputians.

There must have been a thousand of them, lined up

around me in ranks. Behind them I caught a glimpse of little houses, shacks of wood and brick. It was like another miniature city in here – a shanty town, anyway.

But that wasn't the most important thing.

The most important thing was that the Lilliputians all had their bows and arrows drawn, and were aiming at me.

'Now, wait a minute—'

From a thousand bows, a thousand pin-sized arrows flew at me!

CHAPTER FIVE

LILLIPUTIANS

The arrows rose up in a cloud, like little insects. I cried out, and raised my hands to my face, to protect my eyes.

A couple of the arrows lodged in the backs of my hands. They were like tiny pinpricks. But most of the arrows sailed over my head and shoulders.

I saw, now, that the arrows were trailing ropes – Lilliputian ropes, as fine as thread.

Soon I was caught up in hundreds of ropes that crisscrossed my body.

The Lilliputians ran forward, shouting. They were only a few centimetres high, but there were a thousand of them, and it was *scary*.

They started dragging at the ropes. I was off balance. It only took a couple of seconds.

I fell backwards, dragged down. I was so tangled up I could hardly move.

I hit the ground. The Websuit wouldn't let me get bruised, of course, but it didn't stop the wind getting knocked out of me.

The Lilliputians swarmed all over me. It was like having warm little locusts clambering on my body. I heard rapid hammering, like woodpeckers working all around me.

The Lilliputians were nailing the ropes to the ground, so I would be trapped.

I could feel them tugging at my hair. I tried to twist my head, but it was too late.

They had even tied my hair to the floor!

When I was firmly fixed, the Lilliputians climbed off me and backed away.

I was stuck on my back.

Above me, there was a blue glow. At first I thought it was a skylight, but it was rippling.

It was the lake we'd fallen through. It was a thin sheet of water, spread like a roof above me. It looked like the surface of a swimming pool from underwater.

I heard a low sobbing, coming from a couple of metres to my right. I couldn't move my head to see, but I knew who it was. After all, I'd made him cry often enough. That's a big sister's job.

'Byte,' I said. '*Byte.*'

The crying stopped, but he didn't reply.

'*George,*' I said. 'It's me, Sarah.'

'Sarah?'

'Are you OK?'

'They tied me to the floor.' He sounded thoroughly fed up. 'Where's the Wire?'

'I think she's still in the park. She didn't follow us. Listen, Byte. There's nothing to be afraid of. None of this is real.'

'These strings feel real.'

'But they aren't.' I knew it was all just Webware. The Lilliputians had just added restricting commands to the Webware programs that generated my body . . .

How do you explain that to an eight-year-old?

'Listen, Byte. I'm not sure what's happening here, but it's OK. We can't come to any harm.'

'I want to go home,' he whined.

It didn't seem a bad idea. 'All right,' I whispered. 'Just press your scuttle button and you'll be right there. Can you reach it?'

After a few seconds, he wailed, 'No! I can't reach it!'

I tried too. My hands were tied down too firmly. Strain as I might I couldn't break any threads.

It's surprising how strong a thousand thin threads can be.

Something tickled my hair. I thought I could hear giggling.

But I wasn't interested in that. I was starting to get *seriously* annoyed.

I started to shout. 'Hello! Hello! Whoever's there, this is illegal. You aren't allowed to stop us scuttling . . .'

'I don't know why we don't just ask that nice Glumdalclitch to come and help,' Byte said.

I scoffed. 'Your giant girlfriend? Don't be so silly, Byte—'

I could feel bird-like footsteps on my chest.

I managed to look down, past my nose. There was Clefven, standing just beneath my chin, looking at me. A Lilliputian woman stood with him, dressed in a long, old-fashioned skirt. Clefven looked concerned.

Suddenly, he leaned forward and shouted past my ear. 'Hey! Get out of there!'

That giggling behind me got louder, and the tickling in my hair went away.

'Sorry about that,' said Clefven. 'That was Clustril and Drunlo. My kids. They were playing hide-and-seek in your hair.'

'Kids! *Children?* You have children?'

'Yes,' he said. 'And this is my wife, Skyresh.'

The woman glared at me. 'I wish I could say I was pleased to meet you,' she said frostily.

'Hold on a minute,' I said. 'Now I really am confused. You people are phaces. You're not real. You're generated by the computers. You're just part of the scenery in here. You don't have husbands and wives and children!'

He looked amused. 'Well, there you are, Skyresh,' he said. 'We'll just have to get divorced.'

She looked at me. 'I think you'll have to tell her the whole story.'

He sighed. 'I suppose so. Things can't get any worse.' He stood before me. 'Then we'll decide what to do about you.'

'And me,' Byte said miserably.

'Yes, and you.'

I asked, 'What whole story?'

He leaned on his bow. 'Metaphor, we aren't really phaces. I lied to you, I'm afraid.'

'Then you're avatars of real people. In Websuits, out in Realworld somewhere.

'Not that either. Metaphor, we don't exist outside the Web. We are Web creatures. *But we are alive.*'

'That's impossible.'

He laughed again. He put his hand on his chest. 'Well, it doesn't feel impossible. I'm as alive as you are. I can think, and feel, and talk, and love. Just as you can. It's just that I live my whole life inside the Web.'

'But what *are* you?'

'Do you know what computer viruses are?'

I tried to nod, then yelped as the threads pulled at my hair. 'Infections of computer programs.'

'That's how it started, thirty or forty years ago. Viruses eat other programs, and survive, and hide, and breed . . . Exactly what living things do! Metaphor, viruses have had decades to evolve, here inside the Web. At some point, we became aware. Intelligent.'

'We? You're telling me *you* are a computer virus?'

'A descendant of one, yes. We infested these forms, the bodies of Lilliputians inside GulliverZone, because nobody notices us that way.' He laughed. 'The struldbrugs dare not harm us out of doors, because the visitors think we're toys. And nobody takes you seriously, when you're small.'

I grunted. 'Tell me about it. Why don't you just make yourselves big?'

'We can't,' Clefven said. 'But we do have magic dust to shrink things to our size. It's a useful way for us to get equipment.'

Magic dust. Of course he meant size control programs.

'But,' he said, 'we don't have anything to make us grow again. Only Golbasta, the Empress of Lilliput, has that.'

I wondered why she would need such a thing. 'But why hide as Lilliputians? Why don't you want anyone to notice you?'

Now Skyresh came clumping forward to glare at me. 'Because people try to hunt us down.'

'It's true,' Clefven said sadly. 'We're *viruses*. People think we're destructive, even though we haven't been for decades. Nobody wants us. They think we're a waste of mips. So they hound us. That's why we have to hide in places like this, unused parts of the simulations.'

'Who hunts you? The Webcops?'

'Yes,' said Skyresh, 'but they aren't the threat. *Golbasta* is the real danger.'

The Empress again. Why should she hunt Lilliputians?

I still had more questions than answers!

Clefven said, 'The struldbrugs. The beetle-like creatures. You should know about them. They aren't really maintenance routines. That's a cover. They are *familiars*. Golbasta's creatures. Keep out of their way.' He looked sad. 'I'm afraid they took away your friend—'

'The Wire? She isn't really my friend . . . Where did they take her?'

'To the Imperial Court,' Clefven said. 'Look, I think you've heard enough,' he said seriously. 'We have to decide what to do next. We can't just let you go.'

'Oh, we wouldn't tell anyone,' I said.

Skyresh frowned. 'How could we trust you? We have *children* here. I don't want to go on the run again.'

I opened my mouth to protest. I was sincere. I didn't have anything against these Lilliputians, alive or not . . .

But then, it was all taken out of our hands.

Big black shapes clustered on the other side of the pond roof. There was a flash of blue light.

A dozen struldbrugs came splashing through the pond, falling straight towards me!

CHAPTER SIX

STRULDBRUGS

The struldbrugs clattered to the ground all around me. They hit the floor with heavy, leathery thumps, like dropped suitcases.

Skyresh screamed and clung to Clefven. All around me, I could hear the yells of fleeing Lilliputians.

Clefven said, 'We have to get out of here! The struldbrugs must have seen Metaphor and Byte come through. Now the struldbrugs know where we are, we won't be safe from Golbasta.'

'The children!'

'Find them. Bring them here.' They ran to the edge of my chest, and Clefven leaned forward to help Skyresh slither to the ground. She slipped out of my sight. I could hear her little heels clattering over the floor as she ran away.

Clefven got out his bow and arrow. He ran up on to my forehead, over my cheeks. His boots were sharp little points on my skin. 'It's awful,' he said. 'The struldbrugs are everywhere. Skyresh is right. We have to go . . . Oh, no. *Reldresal*.' He lifted up his bow and arrow, pointing it to my left.

'Who's Reldresal? Clefven, tell me.'

He didn't reply. He jumped down off my chest, to my right. He started popping up and down, firing arrows past me.

He was using *me* as cover! And I was still stuck there, unable to move a finger.

I could hear Byte crying.

'Byte!' I called.

He sniffled. 'I'm not frightened.'

He is such a liar. But how could I stop him being frightened? I racked my brains.

'Byte,' I said at last, desperately. 'Isn't this fun?'

He was silent for a minute. 'Fun. Are you kidding?'

'No! This is all part of the theme park. Didn't you know?'

'It is?'

'Of course it is. This is the, uh, the Lair of the Lilliputians. And this is the part where the struldbrugs break in. It's all just a game. Didn't you read the brochure? You weren't really *scared*, were you?'

'It's all just pretend?'

I tried to ignore the screams of the Lilliputians. 'Of course it is.'

'I wasn't scared. I was worried about *you*. I thought *you* were scared.'

For the first time in my life, I was glad to hear him lying.

But now, I could hear something approaching from my left side: an awful slurp and scrape, insectile, powerful, implacable. On my right, Clefven was still popping up and down, firing his arrows, apparently to no avail.

Have you ever had one of those nightmares where the monster is coming, and you can't even move? Being tied down on that floor, at that moment, was *exactly* like that!

The noise came closer and closer, slithering and rattling and sucking.

At last I couldn't stand it any more.

I gritted my teeth, and twisted my head. There was a horrible ripping sound, and I could feel the hair being pulled out of my head in great handfuls.

'Ouch!'

Of course it wasn't *really* my hair. It was just the hair of my avatar, in the Web. But the *pain* was real enough, even though it faded quickly.

My head was free.

I glanced to my right. I saw Clefven with his bow and arrow. Behind him, the struldbrugs were swarming all over the Lilliputians' lair, their big black carapaces gleaming in the watery light from the lake above. They chomped their way busily through the warren. They were crushing houses, even ripping up the floor.

There were Lilliputians everywhere, running between the advancing struldbrugs and screaming. Some of them were trying to fight, but their arrows and little stick swords just bounced off the struldbrugs' shiny backs.

One struldbrug had taken hold of a Lilliputian, a young man. I could see the little fellow squirming in that steely grip, still fighting. But he had no chance. The struldbrug was simply too big for him.

The struldbrug looked like a cat with a bird in its jaw.

The struldbrugs were going to *win*, I realized.

'Wow!' Byte said. 'These special effects are great, Sarah! What a ride!'

There was a fresh scraping close by my left ear.

I turned my head. It was a struldbrug; bigger and blacker than any I'd seen before.

And it had a human face.

It was a woman's face, thin and cold-eyed. She had no teeth in her black mouth. Her head was suspended on the end of a thin struldbrug neck. I could see she had the usual metallic-looking struldbrug legs and mandibles, but she also had two human arms, sticking out in front of her carapace.

Behind me, Clefven shouted, 'Get away from her, Reldresal!'

The struldbrug-woman, Reldresal, smiled at me. 'Don't worry, my dear.' Her voice buzzed like dragonfly wings. 'I won't harm you. I know you're human. I only want those Lilliputians. They're *viruses*, you know.'

'Don't believe her!' Clefven shouted. 'She'll hurt you, Metaphor.'

Looking at Reldresal, I believed him.

'It's all very well telling me that,' I hissed at Clefven, 'but I can't get away anyhow. Can't you cut these ropes?'

He got out a knife – it was a little penknife the size of a fly's wing. He unfolded the blade and began sawing.

When he saw how long it was taking, Byte started shouting at Reldresal. He called her names that would have got him into a *lot* of trouble if Philip had been there. I shouted at him to stop, but he wouldn't and it was working: Reldresal was hesitating, hissing, turning between Byte and myself, wondering who to chomp up first.

I have to admit that must have taken a lot of guts. The little one-mip.

At last Clefven cut one of the ropes on my arm. But it made no difference. I still couldn't move the arm. And there were three hundred more ropes to go!

'It's no good,' I said. 'It's going to take too long. Can't you get some help?'

But then Skyresh ran up. She had two Lilliputian children with her, a boy and a girl. The girl waved at me. Her head barely came up to my nose. Was it only minutes ago that these two kids had been playing hide-and-seek in my hair?

Skyresh said, 'We have to go. *Now*. You can't be worried about *her*. If she hadn't come blundering through the lake, none of this would have happened. Leave her!'

Clefven looked at me, and spread his hands. 'I'm sorry. I can't get you free anyhow . . .'

There was a pressure on my chest, on the left. I looked that way.

It was Reldresal. She was climbing over me! Her mandibles waved in my face, like little knives. 'Don't worry,' she said. '*I'll* cut you free.' Her voice was like a snake's hiss.

When I looked back, Clefven was backing away regretfully.

I had to think of something, and fast, or – in some way I still didn't understand – Byte and I were going to be a struldbrug's breakfast!

'Wait,' I said. 'The magic dust! Clefven, do you have any?'

He stopped.

Skyresh said, 'Come *on*.'

But Clefven patted a pouch at his belt. 'Yes. Why?'

'Shrink us! It's the only way!'

He shook his head. 'We've never tried it on the avatar of a real person. It might be dangerous.'

Reldresal was climbing further up my chest. I could feel her hard weight. 'We don't have a choice. Please, Clefven.'

He came running back to me. He dug out a tiny handful of dust from the pouch and threw it over my face. It was blue, and it sparkled like Christmas tree glitter. Then he went running over to Byte, out of my sight.

It took a second to work. Reldresal's face loomed closer to mine . . .

I started to shrink.

Shrinking feels like falling.

Reldresal's face seemed to rise upwards, away from me, as if I was falling down a well. And the pressure of the ropes slackened. Soon I was able to start squeezing out of them.

But I kept shrivelling, getting smaller and smaller.

I stood up. I was surrounded by heaps of thick ropes, stacked up taller than I was. They were the threads that had tied me up, I realized. I was the same size as Clefven – in fact, shorter. And here came Byte, reduced to the same scale as me, running towards me.

'Look at me! Look at me!' he shouted.

He tripped on a rope and went flat on his face. It was just so *typical*.

All the while, far above us, I could see the huge shining belly of Reldresal, the struldbrug-woman, as she worked her way over the ropes, looking for me.

Clefven was back with his family. Now I was the same size, they looked like real people. He grinned at me. 'You'll be safe now.'

'Yes. Go, Clefven. Thank you.'

The Lilliputian family ran off.

I lifted up the control pad on my wrist. 'Get ready to scuttle,' I told Byte. 'You remember how?'

'Aw,' he said. 'I'm having *fun*.'

'Just do it, one-mip!'

I raised my hand to my own scuttle button.

I waited, just for a moment, before pressing it – the way you might wait before taking your first bite of an ice-cream, just to draw out the anticipation.

It was *such* a relief, and I wallowed in the feeling. I was as good as safe already! In just seconds I would be out of here, and home. There was still the Wire to think about, but I was sure once I told Philip what had happened, and he spoke to the Webcops, it would soon be sorted out.

'Ready?' I said to Byte.

He lifted his hand to his scuttle button.

'Three, two, one—' We both pressed.

Nothing happened. I was still in that dusty wooden cavern. Byte was still here too, looking confused.

The scuttle buttons didn't work!

And now Reldresal had seen us. Her face was like a huge

white cloud above us. Her mandible was reaching for us, like the blade of a mechanical digger.

But that wasn't the true horror of the moment for me. We were still stuck here, in the bowels of GulliverZone – *with no way home!*

CHAPTER SEVEN

HUNTED

I grabbed Byte's hand and pulled him aside.

Reldresal's mandible came clattering down on the ground, just behind us.

I ran after Clefven, jumping over the discarded ropes.

'I thought we were going home,' Byte said, panting as I yanked him along.

'Oh, let's stay a bit more.'

'Yay!' He was pleased.

I never thought I'd be glad about my brother's total lack of brain.

I looked up as we ran. I could see Reldresal's face casting to and fro. Her huge shining belly slid over us like a roof.

There were, I decided, advantages to being small. Reldresal obviously had trouble seeing us.

There were very few Lilliputians left now. Evidently everyone had either been swept up by the struldbrugs, or had run off. But the Lilliputians' lair was still full of struldbrugs. They looked like huge machines, giant tanks on legs, picking over the ruins of a town. It wouldn't take them long to find us. And then . . .

I didn't know what would happen. But I was sure it wouldn't be pleasant!

But how could we escape? I couldn't have reached back up to that lake in the roof, even when I was my normal size. And now it was just impossible.

I spotted Clefven. He was shepherding his family into

what looked like the mouth of a well dug into the floor.
The two children and then Skyresh dropped through the
little black circle, and each time there was a flash of blue
light.

The struldbrugs were very close. Clefven was about to
jump into the well.

'Clefven!' I called. 'Wait!'

He stopped, on the rim of the well. 'You're all right. I'm
glad.'

'Is that a way out?'

He hesitated. Poor Clefven was so late because he had
stayed behind to help us. He'd put his family at risk for us.
And now, I was asking him to do the same again.

'Yes. Come on. Hurry. The struldbrugs can't follow, it's
too narrow.'

The hole was just a bottomless black disc in the ground. I
had no idea where it led to.

Would *you* just jump in?

I saw a struldbrug approaching, legs clattering mech-
anically.

'Hurry,' hissed Clefven.

I pushed Byte into the hole. He disappeared in a blue
flash.

'Now you,' said Clefven.

I closed my eyes and jumped.

Even through my closed eyelids I could see electric blue.

Byte, the dummy, was standing under me as I came
through. I fell right on top of him.

We fell over on coarse grass.

I looked around. We were underneath a wooden roof, a
metre or so above my head – no, I reminded myself, now I
was only ten centimetres tall! It must have been only five
centimetres above, half my height. Beyond the roof, a few
paces away, the grass continued on to a sunlit lawn.

I pulled Byte out of the way. In a few seconds, Clefven came through. It was as if he was falling through a trapdoor. But when I looked up, I could see nothing but solid wooden roof.

He brushed himself off, and smiled at us. He was now about as tall as Philip in relation to me, though he couldn't have weighed so much.

I felt embarrassed to think I'd picked him up like a toy and just carried him into that lake without even asking him. Because he was small, I hadn't taken him seriously. I, of all people, should know better than that!

'We're safe now,' he said. 'For the time being. Come on.'

He led us out into sunshine. Looking back, I saw that we'd come out of the empty bandstand in the middle of the Mildendo park.

Skyresh and the children were waiting. The children came running up to Clefven, who hugged them. Skyresh just glared at me. I couldn't blame her.

I looked around. Everything seemed *huge* – even though it was, of course, all scaled to my size. The city wall, that I'd scrambled over earlier, was now a formidable barrier, like the wall around a prison. Those miniature oak trees now looked huge and old. The lake, a little way away, was immense, with big yachts tacking back and forth on its surface.

Even the grass under my feet was coarse and a little overgrown.

Byte was looking at the lake, puzzled.

'Don't strain your brain, you little egg.'

'I was just thinking,' he said slowly. 'We fell *down* through the lake – and then we fell *down* out of the bandstand. But we ended up in the same place we came from. We didn't climb any stairs – did we?'

I sighed. 'Look, Webtown is different from Realworld.

Mostly it obeys the same laws. But it doesn't have to because it's all just made up by computers. See?'

He frowned, trying to be adult, but I could see he was faking it.

'Some day I'll take you to EscherLand . . . Oh, never mind.' I wiggled my fingers in his face. '*It's magic*. Just accept it.'

Now the two children, Drunlo and Clustril, had come up to Byte and were staring at him curiously. They were about his age, I suppose.

Within about one second the three of them had started to play catch.

Within two more seconds they were fighting.

Kids!

Clefven was standing with his arm around Skyresh. She seemed angry and upset, but he was more resigned.

'What will you do now?' I asked.

'We'll be all right.' Clefven smiled tiredly. 'We have many places to hide. Not even the struldbrugs have found them all yet. But what about you?' he asked. 'I thought you would scuttle home.'

'We tried. The buttons didn't work.'

'Oh.' He nodded. 'I told you the dust wasn't designed for real people. It must have damaged your Websuits.'

I frowned. I thought I understood. Probably because of the different scales, our scuttle buttons were sending out differently pitched signals – the way a penny whistle makes a higher sound than a recorder – which the big computers controlling Webtown couldn't recognize.

'It's OK,' I said breezily. 'All you have to do is grow us again, and we'll be able to get out.'

Clefven looked solemn. 'I told you. We don't have growth dust. Only Golbasta, the Empress, has that.'

Golbasta.

I could see her palace, on the horizon of the park. It had

looked like a pretty dolls' house before. Now it looked more like a forbidding Norman castle.

For the first time Skyresh looked genuinely concerned for us. 'I'm sorry. I know none of this was your fault. You must be very frightened. Look, why don't you stay with us? We'll show you where to hide and how to live. It isn't so bad, being a Lilliputian.'

I shook my head. 'Thanks. But that isn't possible. You see, we're not really here . . .' I told her about home, our real bodies in our Websuits in the spare room. Clefven nodded. 'We can only stay here for two or three hours. Otherwise we'll start to get Websick.'

Skyresh asked, 'Websickness? What's that?'

'You get it if you wear your suit for too long. You see, we aren't really moving around, although it looks as if we are . . . No matter what we do in the Web, our bodies are just lying still, out there in Realworld. It's a sort of gap, you see. After a while it catches up with you, and your body can't cope.'

'Then you must go to the palace,' Clefven said firmly. 'Only the Empress has the dust to grow you again. And besides, that's where your friend the Wire was taken.'

'But how can we get there? And even if we make it, will the Empress just give the dust to us?'

Clefven and Skyresh looked at each other mournfully.

They didn't have to say anything. From what I'd seen of her familiars, the struldbrugs, Golbasta wasn't going to help us. The very opposite, in fact.

And yet, what choice was there?

It had become very dark.

Suddenly, there was an explosion on the roof of the bandstand. Then another one.

A huge flattened ball of liquid landed in the grass a few feet from me. Water splashed everywhere.

Clefven and Skyresh reacted immediately. 'Drunlo! Clustril! Indoors, right now!'

The children came scurrying to the bandstand, holding their hands over their heads.

I called, 'You'd better come too, Byte.'

He looked confused. He came, but slower than the others.

Then a huge ball of water came down from nowhere and smashed him in the shoulder-blades. He fell over, howling.

I ran forward, grabbed him by the collar and pulled him to his feet. Volleys of water were pounding the grass flat all around us.

We made it to the grandstand. Clefven and his family were already huddled there. Byte was soaked.

I asked, 'What's that? The struldbrugs?'

Skyresh was puzzled. 'No. Just rain.'

'*Rain?*'

Clefven said, 'Not everything is Lilliputian-sized here. You have to be careful.'

Skyresh said, 'Sometimes it hails. It's like being pelted with tennis balls.'

She didn't say any more, but I could see in her face how serious she was. The Lilliputians weren't wearing Websuits that would shield them from pain. They were *really* here – in a manner of speaking, anyway. Hailstones the size of tennis balls would *hurt*.

Byte was soaked, and miserable again. I tried to get the worst of it out of his hair. Philip had trusted me to look after Byte. A fine job I was making of it.

If we couldn't even cope with the rain, how could I hope to make it to the Imperial Court and challenge Golbasta?

It seemed impossible. I felt pitifully small, over-whelmed by everything.

And we were alone.

I don't think I've ever felt more depressed in my life.

CHAPTER EIGHT

GIANTS

Clefven turned to Skyresh. 'I think we should help them.' In that moment, he looked more like Philip than ever.

Skyresh bit her lip and looked at her bedraggled, bewildered children. 'Yes,' she said. 'All right. We can't just abandon them. They're only kids themselves.'

I bridled a bit at that, but it was not the moment to argue!

'And besides,' Clefven said, 'maybe it's time we challenged Golbasta. She's had it her own way too long.' He turned to me. 'I'll take you to the palace.'

'Clefven, thank you. I—'

He was gruff. 'Thank me when we've made it. I only hope I'm not leading you into greater danger.'

He moved deeper inside the bandstand. There was a little pile of gear: swords, bows and arrows. Clefven pulled out a sword. At least, I thought it was a sword. It was actually a darning needle, just a pillar of steel with a sharpened edge and an eye at the end. But we were so small now it looked half a metre long! Clefven tucked it into his belt.

He turned to Skyresh and kissed her cheek. Then he knelt down and hugged his children.

'Come back safely,' Skyresh said. 'We need you.' She was crying.

I was nearly crying myself. To think I'd thought these people were just little dolls!

Clefven led us out of the bandstand. Drunlo and Clustril stood with their mother and waved to us.

'Come on,' said Clefven. 'To the palace!'

We started to walk across the park, towards the imposing walls of the Imperial Court.

'The thing to remember,' said Clefven,. 'is that you're not humans for the time being. *You're Lilliputians.* And things are different for us.'

'I understand,' I said. 'The rain—'

'Not just that. Remember, nobody takes us seriously. People think we're toys, or worse. Vermin.' He glanced about. 'The struldbrugs shouldn't bother us out in the open. But be careful. Reldresal is their leader. She would recognize you again. And there are many other dangers.'

Byte tugged my hand. He had dried out, and he was mutating back into a hideous little brother again. 'That lady called you a kid,' he taunted. 'Kid, kid!'

I grabbed him and we began a ritual wrestle. I have to admit I enjoyed it, and I tried to do him less damage than usual. It was a little bit of home in a strange place.

There was a loud buzzing sound.

Clefven called, 'Metaphor. Watch out!'

We broke our clinch and looked at each other. 'Is that you?' I accused Byte.

'Is not. It's *you.*'

'*Look out!*'

The buzzing got louder. Something came swooping out of the sky at me. I thought it was a bird.

It was coming right at my head!

I ducked, and pulled Byte's head into my belly.

I looked up. The 'bird' had fluttering translucent wings, a body striped yellow and black, black goggle eyes, and a sting protruding from its tail . . .

That 'bird' was a wasp, half as big as I was.

It came straight at me again. I screamed and hunched over Byte.

It landed on me! I could feel its sticky feet on my back. In any moment it would sting me . . .

I heard a swishing noise. The buzzing stopped.

Cautiously, I stood up straight.

Clefven was standing there, needle-sword in hand. The wasp's body lay at his feet on the grass. Its belly was covered in satiny fur, its legs were twitching, and black glop was oozing from its neck. Clefven had cut the wasp's head clean off. It lay a little way away, like a misshapen black football.

'Wow,' said Byte. 'The special effects here are awesome.'

I breathed out. 'Thanks,' I said.

Clefven grinned. 'Always look up. That's where trouble comes from.' He bent down over the wasp and pulled out its sting. It was a curved needle five centimetres long. 'Here,' he said. 'A souvenir of GulliverZone.'

I took it, and threw it as far from me as possible. 'No thanks.'

'Oh, poor little things. Did you have trouble with a nasty wasp? Oh, dear. Oh, they are so *sweet* . . .'

This barrage of baby-talk was coming from above my head. I looked up . . . to see a huge, sandalled foot coming down out of the sky, right on top of Byte.

Clefven grabbed him and pulled him out of the way.

I don't know what damage that would have done. Normally a Websuit won't let you come to any real harm.

But this wasn't normal. Our Websuits weren't meant to work like this. I didn't want to run any experiments I didn't have to!

'Oh, look at the little one. It's so *dinky*.'

I looked up. Two mountainous ladies stood over us. They were like two office buildings walking around on sandalled feet, draped in garish summer dresses that were much too young for them.

They were *not* underweight.

The ladies were leaning down at us. Their smiling, chubby faces were like two huge moons in the sky. Their voices sounded like thunder, far above us.

Clefven ignored the ladies. 'Come on . . .'

'Wait,' I said, suddenly excited.

'What?'

'These are adults. They can help us get out of here.' I didn't know why I hadn't thought of it before. It was obvious! This was still just a theme park, after all, Golbasta or no Golbasta.

I leaned back and shouted. 'Excuse me. Down here!' I waved.

The ladies pursed their mouths in little O shapes.

'Mildred – I think she's speaking to us!'

'Isn't it marvellous? The things they do nowadays.'

'Can you help me? We're stuck here. We shouldn't be this size. And now our scuttle buttons don't work.'

They tutted.

'Oh, dear.'

'Fancy that.'

'Will you take a message to my father, please? He's probably still at work. At the Tilbury Desalination Plant. I'm sure he'll know what to do.'

Huge relief filled me. It was all over! All these ladies had to do was find a data-box to send out a message. Once Philip got home, he'd be able to unhook us from the Websuits. The Wire, too.

But the ladies were straightening up. 'How amusing,' one said.

They started walking on!

'Wait!' I called. 'Please! Listen to me!' I jumped up and down, but they didn't look down again.

I heard their voices booming back and forth across the sky.

'So clever. So much *detail*.'

'And those wonderful fantasy games for the children. *Father* indeed! It's a shame we're a little too old to play, Mildred . . .'

And they just walked away, like two receding ocean liners.

I walked back to Clefven. Byte looked confused.

'I'm sorry,' Clefven said. 'But I did warn you. Nobody takes us seriously. The visitors think we're just toys. Part of the scenery. They don't even know we're *alive*.'

'But it's obvious we're alive!'

He shrugged. 'Did you think *I* was alive?'

He had a point.

We walked on.

We rounded a glade of big oak trees. Byte was still happy, in his ignorance. He ran ahead, using up his energy. He ran around the corner of the glade, out of our sight.

Byte screamed!

Your kid brother screaming really is a horrible sound. It makes your blood run cold.

Clefven and I ran around the corner. I actually beat Clefven.

Byte was standing, frozen to the ground.

And, facing him, a black cat was treating him to a blank, piercing stare.

I remembered we'd seen this cat when we arrived. But now it was the size of a Tyrannosaurus Rex, and it towered over poor Byte!

The cat took a delicate step forward, staring straight at

my brother. It was just a phace, of course. Just another situation. It wouldn't hurt us. It *couldn't* hurt us. But—

It looked hungry.

CHAPTER NINE

ANIMAL

Byte was whimpering. 'Is this another game?'

'Yes. Just another game. This is, uh, the Big Cat Challenge . . .'

The cat took another step forward. Two more paces and it would grab my little brother like a sparrow.

I hissed to Clefven. 'Surely it won't hurt him. The programming—'

He shook his head. 'If you stay around here for long, you'll find that not everything is as it seems. Sure it's a phace, but if you're our size, you ought to think of it as if it's a real cat. And think what a real cat would do to you. Your brother's suit might not protect him.'

'Then it's up to me.' I was scared to death, but I took a step forward.

The cat turned its head towards me. Its flat face was like a big radar dish, sweeping down at me, and I could see myself reflected in its black eyes. I looked so *small*.

Clefven put his hand on my arm. 'Remember, think *real* cat.'

'So what?'

'So, use some cat psychology.'

Psychology.

I thought of how Gazza, our fat cat, behaves around unfamiliar animals.

The worst thing to do would be to show fear. I walked

towards the cat, past Byte. 'It's all right,' I told him. 'You just stay where you are.' And I walked on, right up to the head of the cat.

It loomed over me like a gigantic sculpture.

I walked back and forth, five or six times, staring up at the cat. 'You see?' I said. 'I'm not scared of you.'

It watched me, fascinated and nervous. It drew its head back and forth as I walked, tracking my movements. It had its claws out – every one as thick as my wrist – but it didn't look as if it was going to spring.

A Lilliputian bird fluttered over my head. To the cat the little phace must have looked the size of a fly.

The cat lost interest in me immediately. It leaped up with frightening speed and strength, and ran off after the bird.

Clefven came up to me. 'Well done,' he said. 'The animals are bigger and heavier than you, but you're smarter. You can't out-fight them but you can out-think them.'

Byte came up, grinning. 'So that's the secret of the Big Cat Challenge. *Venomous*.'

'Yes,' I said. 'Venomous.'

I was trembling.

I walked on towards the palace. Maybe the cat had been truly dangerous, maybe not. I just hoped the others wouldn't notice how scared I was!

At the heart of Mildendo there are a set of barriers surrounding the palace itself. There are the walls of the Imperial Court, then the moat, and beyond that the giant crèche, the place they store the babies.

They hadn't struck me as barriers when we'd first arrived – when we were visitors – but they sure felt like barriers now, and no doubt that's how they were designed. I had no idea how we'd get across that moat, for instance.

But first we had to cross the crèche.

The crèche was surrounded by a fence, presumably to keep out us pesky Lilliputians, and keep the babies in. But there was a stile over the fence.

Every step came up to my waist, and there were twenty-five of them.

We started to climb. I felt exhausted by the time we got to the top.

There were perhaps a dozen giants – that is, normal-sized adults! – sitting around here at tables. And there must have been forty or fifty babies, all giant-sized, waddling around the crèche area, colliding with each other, gurgling like air-raid sirens and grabbing wildly at huge shiny toys. In their garish dungarees and caps they looked like carnival blimps. And every chin was coated with a river of drool.

What a nightmare!

I know not everyone agrees about putting young kids in Websuits. One year old is the legal lower age limit. It does get them used to using the equipment, even if they can't do much when they are in there except play with the kind of toys they get in Realworld anyhow. It's a bit like taking a small child to learn to swim. They can't cross the Channel, but they get used to the water.

I don't care one way or the other about babies in Websuits. I'm old enough to have watched Byte grow up, and frankly the whole thing was a shuddering nightmare. As far as I'm concerned every baby should be put in a box, Websuit and all, until it is civilized enough to be able to ask to come out, and say *please*.

So you can imagine how I felt as I watched those gibbering giants waddle around the crèche – an area I was going to have to cross to reach the Imperial Court!

At least nobody had noticed us. I felt as if I had turned into a rat, or a sparrow, perched up there on the fence.

One of the tables had been pushed up against the fence. It was piled up with building blocks and toys.

'Come on,' Clefven said. 'It might be easier to get down that way.'

He led the way along the top of the fence. It was just a single thickness of wood, but it was a good arm's length wide. We jumped down perhaps half my height to the tabletop. We walked across the table. There was a plastic padded tablecloth covered with huge grinning TFO ostrich faces, so soft and thick it was easy to trip up on a ruck.

Up close to normal-sized stuff, everything was so *big*. On the table there was a plastic plate with green toy slime on it where some little angel had been playing at cooking. I counted – it took me twenty-four paces to walk past the plate. There was a toy teacup the size of a barrel. In the middle of the tea party stuff there was a bright blue inflatable boat with a limp sail and a soppy grinning sailor boy, a bit bigger than I was. We came to a bright red plastic knife. Byte climbed up on it and started using the blade as a diving board, until I told him off for getting too close to the sharp edge.

We reached the edge of the table.

It was like being on top of a small flat-roofed building. The grass looked an awfully long way down.

'Come on,' Clefven said. 'We can climb down the tablecloth.'

He got down on his belly and squirmed backwards until his feet stuck out over the edge of the table. He hooked his feet into rucks in the cushioned plastic, and started using it like a rope ladder.

He looked back up at us. 'Easy,' he said. 'You next, Byte, then your sister.'

The little egg loved it, of course. He just swarmed down.

I went a little more cautiously, as befitted my age. And my fear of heights. But it was easy, really.

At the bottom, the grass loomed up around us like shoots of green bamboo.

There was a toy close by, a little round fat clown. When I got close enough to trigger it, it smiled and started singing in a screeching roar, 'Hello, little girl. Would you like to hear a song? *Daisy, Daisy, give me your answer do . . .*'

Byte had had this toy. I always hated it. I always hated that song! And now here it was, come back to haunt me, bigger than I was.

I kicked it until it rolled away and shut up. It was a waste of time, of course, but it felt *good*!

There was a shattering roar.

Somewhere above us, two babies were approaching each other, cooing like dinosaurs bellowing across a primeval swamp.

They hadn't seen us.

We crouched down in the grass while two pairs of stumpy legs came crashing down like pink tree-trunks, flattening the grass around us. If they stepped in the wrong place, we would – maybe – have been squashed like bugs.

With unintelligible gurgles, the two infant monsters tottered away.

We straightened up. 'This isn't so bad,' I said. 'All we have to do is avoid being stepped on. Now, we have to think about how to get across the moat—'

'Look out!'

I spun around.

I glimpsed a huge face, a flat bald forehead, a wide grin and teeth the size of our front door. A giant pudgy pink hand came sweeping down from nowhere and grabbed me around the middle. I was swept up in the air before I knew what was happening.

I heard a hideous cooing.

It was a baby.
No, that doesn't do it justice.
It was a BABY!

CHAPTER TEN

BABY

The baby's fat right hand was big enough to close around my waist. It (the baby was a boy, but all babies are *it* as far as I'm concerned) was dragging me across the ground. My arms were pinned to my sides. The breath was squeezed out of me like toothpaste out of a tube. Spots of blackness gathered across my vision.

When the baby felt me wriggling, it squeezed tighter, so hard I thought I could feel my ribs grinding over each other!

Now it pulled me right into its chest. The coarse wet bristly fabric of its bib – soaked in drool, of course – rubbed against my face. I was only glad I couldn't smell anything . . .

It did me no good at all to know that none of this was *real*! The baby was in its own little Websuit in some hideous pink-walled nursery somewhere. And I was writhing around in my own home. What shouldn't be happening was that this was *hurting*.

It relaxed its grip a little and suddenly I could breathe again.

Now there was a moist scrape against my cheek. It made me shudder. The baby was stroking the side of my face with a finger of its other hand. The skin was soft, but it poked so hard it hurt. But it was trying to be gentle, I figured.

I tried not to struggle in case it tightened up again.

It lifted me off the ground.

It scraped my face against the soft fat on its lower chin. The skin there was soaked with dribble, so my face was soon drenched . . . *Ugh*. If you want to know what that experience was like, go open a three-day-old garbage pail and push your face into the mushy, moist stuff at the bottom.

I had had an all-round bad day, but this was the pits! It was all the nightmares I'd ever had, during those years with Byte as a kid brother, come to hideous, bloated life.

Things, I thought, can't get any worse.

And then – of course – they did.

The baby lifted me up higher and held me before its gaping mouth. They were only milk teeth, I suppose, but they were like a row of ceramic guillotines, closing around my neck!

I squeezed my eyes shut.

But my head stayed on my shoulders.

Seconds later, I risked opening my eyes.

A huge doughnut of pink, puckered-up lip was looming in front of me. The baby rubbed its lips all over my face. It was like having a saliva car-wash.

It was *kissing* me.

I just closed my eyes and mouth and endured it. At least, I comforted myself, it wasn't biting my head off.

'Metaphor!' It was Clefven. 'Are you all right?'

When the baby had done smooching, I turned my head away, gasping for air. 'Oh, terrific. It's not going to eat me, is it?'

He hesitated. 'Of course he can't. But I don't suppose he understands about Websuits. He might try . . .'

I would have laughed if I'd had the breath. After all that preaching I'd had from Philip about being kind to my little brother, I was going to end up as an infant's between-meals snack!

Now Byte was shouting. 'Leave my sister alone!'

Something clattered on the floor near me. It was a giant-sized plastic bead, the size of a football.

Byte was throwing things at the baby.

The baby pointed and said something like, '*Ack-shum-mam. Ach-shum-mam.*'

It thought Byte was an *Action Man*! I groaned. If only he was, I thought. Then he might have been some use all those long years. At least I could have swapped him.

Byte was getting ready to throw again.

Clefven said, 'Byte, no—'

But it was too late. 'Put her down!' And Byte hurled another bead that caught the baby square in one big blue eye.

The baby bared its teeth and screamed so loudly it left my ears ringing. It clutched me to its chest. It started jumping up and down – I was pounded into its hot belly – and then it turned and ran.

It was like being trapped inside a huge, hot, pudgy roller-coaster. With nobody at the controls.

I could hear Clefven calling. 'Psychology! Remember, Metaphor—'

The baby scurried to the table we'd climbed down from. It ran underneath and stood there bawling.

And where, I wanted to know, was its mother?

After a few seconds of that it calmed down. It settled on its haunches close to the tea party plate we'd seen before. It hauled me around in its arms, and I was forced to lie flat against its upper leg with its heavy arm over me like a giant podgy seat-belt. It started stroking my face again, making a strange, almost gentle noise.

It was crooning, I thought.

I thought of what Clefven had said. *Psychology*. He'd

been talking about animals, but believe me, that word sums up all babies, without exception, pretty well.

What was this wretched infant thinking?

Suddenly, I understood. *It was trying to cradle me.*

It thought I was a doll!

I had to reassure it I really was a dolly, I guessed. No threat to it. Otherwise it would throw me over against the fence without even thinking about it.

So what do babies do all day?

I tried to relax so I wasn't lying stiff and resistant in its arms. I looked up at it and smiled. I tried to get eye contact.

Eventually, I thought, it would put me down. Until then, I just had to endure. It would get bored and go to another toy. Maybe it wouldn't be so bad. It was almost comfortable here.

But now a huge pink finger was looming at me out of the sky. It was dripping with green slime.

The baby was going to feed me!

I couldn't help it. I started struggling again and pulled my face away. But it locked my head in the crook of its arm and forced that fingertip into my mouth.

I couldn't taste anything, of course, but I could *feel* that awful cold lumpy plastic slime sploshing over my face and mouth. And if you have ever *seen* that stuff you can imagine what that was like!

'Are you ready, Byte?'

It was Clefven's voice.

'Three, two, one. Go!'

Suddenly, both Clefven and Byte started yelling. I could hear them running at the baby from two sides, making as much noise as they could.

The baby yelped indignantly. It jumped up and dropped me. The grass was spiky but it cushioned my fall.

The baby ran off in a blur of primary colours, looking for its mother.

Clefven and Byte ran up and huddled over me.

Clefven picked lumps of cold slime out of my mouth. 'Are you all right, Metaphor?'

'I think so,' I mumbled around the slime.

'I hoped that would work. I didn't want to scare him too much – just surprise him enough to make him drop you.'

'You *hoped* it would work?'

Byte, sitting on the tablecloth, looked worried. 'That wasn't really a ride, was it?'

I looked into his round, serious little face, and I wondered whether to try keeping up the fiction.

'No,' I said. 'It wasn't a ride.'

'And we're really in trouble here.'

I sat up and took his hand. 'Yes, we are.'

'Then why don't we ask Glumdalclitch to help?'

'I told you. That won't do any good. She's just part of the theme park. She isn't *real*.'

'But she said—'

'Look, don't worry. Clefven is helping us. And we're going to find a way home. OK?'

'Yes,' he said. I could see he wanted to cry, but he was determined not to.

He's not such a bad kid, really. For a one-mip basement-level wipeout little brother, anyhow.

We moved out of the crèche, in towards the centre of Mildendo and the Imperial Court. I thought the next problem we'd face would be getting across the moat.

It wasn't.

We reached the edge of the crèche's long grass. Clefven grabbed our shoulders. 'Wait,' he said, and he pulled us back into the grass a little way.

We heard them before we saw them; a slithering, lizardy, scraping, snakelike sound, utterly inhuman.

A patrol of giant struldbrugs was marching around the paved area between us and the moat. And the lead struldbrug had an eerily beautiful human face.

CHAPTER ELEVEN

RELDRESAL

Our three faces, staring out of the bamboo-length grass, must have looked like three round coins.

The struldbrugs marched past, antennae waving, mandibles clacking. Each of them was about the size of a dog, as I've said, so now they towered over us. Their multi-jointed legs clattered against the pavement.

They were marching in time, I realized after a while. That was an eerie thought. When have you ever seen a column of insects *march in time*, outside of an interactive cartoon?

The column moved slowly, with Reldresal at the front, so I had plenty of time to inspect her. That human face of hers was still there, stuck on the front of the insect body. But I thought I could see some differences. Like a coat of mail shell, the hard black chitin seemed to have progressed a little further up her neck. And her skin looked strangely shiny, as if it was made of wax, or plastic. In the middle of her cheeks and forehead there were small, hard spots of black chitin.

'Her eyes will go next,' whispered Clefven.

'What do you mean?'

'She's turning from a human to a struldbrug,' he said. 'You realize that, don't you? The body is fairly easy to transform. Your arms and legs, and lungs and heart and stomach, are just machines anyhow. They just have to be replaced with other machines.'

'Ugh,' said Byte.

Clefven smiled. 'I didn't say it was nice,' he said. 'Actually it's very painful. It's just easy. But the human brain is the most complex object in the universe. It takes a long time for the struldbrug form to accommodate the head.

'Reldresal will come out of a sleep period soon with eyes like a fly's: lumps of grainy cells . . . It will hurt, because her new eyes won't fit easily into her human skull. But it won't last long. Soon her skull will soften, and start blending into the rest of her new chitin body.'

I inspected the other struldbrugs, as they marched past. They weren't identical, I saw, now that they were so close to me. Reldresal had the most obviously human features – that face. But here and there I could make out other remnants of humanity: a pair of pink hands sticking out of a black chest, what looked like ears on the side of a struldbrug's sketch of a head, even a pair of blue, frightened human eyes peering out from a mask of chitin.

'*They all used to be human*. Didn't they?'

'Every one of them.'

Byte said, 'Why don't they just spin out, and go back to their normal bodies?'

I thought that was a good question, for him. It showed he was starting to understand what was going on here.

'Because they can't,' Clefven said sadly. 'They don't have normal bodies to go back to.'

I didn't understand. 'What do you mean? Are they Websick?'

'Worse than that. They've stayed inside the Web so long, they've let their Realworld bodies wither away. Now, the only way they can survive is by staying inside the Web. Just what you see before you.'

I found myself shivering. It was supposed to be imposs-ible for me to be uncomfortably cold – but that's how I felt.

A lot of things were supposed to be impossible inside the Web, such as getting trapped there. But that was just the fix we were in. And now, I was learning, there were monsters – half-human – inhabiting the corners of the Web too!

Suddenly, the Web seemed a much darker place than I could have imagined.

'If your Empress Golbasta does this to people, she must be really evil. No wonder you're frightened of her.'

'No. You don't understand. Golbasta doesn't *force* people to become Struldbrugs. They *choose* to do it.'

I was mystified. 'How? What do you actually have to do, to become a Struldbrug? Do you have to go somewhere? Eat something?'

He wouldn't tell me. But I noticed he shuddered when I said, *Eat something* . . .

Clefven said, 'People become Struldbrugs, sacrificing everything – even their lives outside the Web – because Golbasta offers them something wonderful.'

'What does she offer? Money? Fame?'

'Toys?' Byte asked.

'Something beyond price. I'm telling you this because if we get caught, no matter what she offers you, you must remember what the *cost* will be.'

I couldn't imagine what could possibly be so wonderful that people were prepared to leave Realworld behind for ever.

But, I thought, what if Golbasta had captured the Wire? What if she made this wonderful offer to *her*? After all, Realworld wasn't such a wonderful place for the Wire. Philip had been right. I *did* know how she felt. The few months after Mum died were the worst of my life. You never really get over that.

If, in the middle of that, somebody had offered me something *wonderful*, I might have taken it.

Meanwhile, I had a lot of unanswered questions on my

plate. How do you become a struldbrug? What did Golbasta offer that made it worth becoming a struldbrug? Why did she want to capture Lilliputians? What did Golbasta *herself* want?

I wondered how many of these questions I would have to answer before we could get home again.

We waited until we were sure we had a long clear period before the struldbrug patrol came back again.

We crept out of the long grass and headed towards the moat. I felt very exposed, out in the open like that. But we knew the struldbrugs were a long way away.

A big black shadow came sweeping across us.

I saw a gigantic figure, silhouetted against the sun, and a huge hand reaching down at me. I thought it must be the baby back again.

But the hand was big and muscular.

A thumb and forefinger closed around my waist, pinching tight. I pushed down at the thumb, trying to get away.

I was hoisted into the air. It was like a bungee jump in reverse! I was held up like a bug, suspended before a huge grinning face. I was small and utterly helpless.

He was wearing a huge red cloak, which looked, from my point of view, as big and heavy as the curtain in a cinema.

I laughed out loud. Immediately I knew we were going to be all right. At last we'd found a normal-sized person who *would* listen to me.

It was Surfer!

CHAPTER TWELVE

SURFER

I tried to wave at him, but my arms were pinned. I kicked my legs. 'Surfer! It's me, Metaphor!'

He held me up in the air before his eyes. I could see myself reflected in those big eyeballs. When I kicked my legs, I saw I looked like a wriggling egg. I felt embarrassed and stopped kicking.

'Wow. You can *talk*?' His voice was a deep boom, like thunder in some remote cloud.

'Of course I can talk. I've been talking since I was two years old.'

He shook me back and forth like a pepper pot, making my legs wave.

'Will you *stop* that?'

'The special effects in here are just a-*mazing*.'

He was pinching me over the kidneys with his big clumsy thumb and finger. 'You're hurting me,' I shouted.

He leaned his head closer to me and turned his ear. It was a great big fleshy sculpture, all caverns and shadows and ridges. 'Your voice is like a wasp buzz. Say something else. Go ahead. Can you sing a song?'

For some reason a tune went through my head: *Daisy, Daisy* . . . 'No, I can't sing a song!' I screamed.

He drew his head back and looked at me seriously for the first time.

'I'm hurting you? Really?'

'Really.' I wriggled, trying to loosen the vice-like grip of his thumb and forefinger.

He held out his other hand and dropped me gently on to it. His palm was firm and warm. Then he picked me up by a pinch of cloth at the scruff of the neck.

'Listen, can I get to keep you?'

'*What?*'

'I've picked up a couple of souvenirs already. Do you know the flying island? They have these wacky scientist geezers who are squeezing the sunlight out of cucumbers and putting it into little bottles. Every time you open the bottle the sun shines out. I put it in my hard drive for a souvenir. Even the gifts are free today . . . So how about it?'

'No, you can't keep me! I'm mine! I belong to me!'

He frowned. 'You know, you look just like that girl I met out in Webtown.'

At last! 'Metaphor. Yes. That's me!'

'But you're a Lilliputian. And Lilliputians aren't real. They're just phaces. Aren't they?'

I'd had enough of this. 'Listen to me, you, you red-cloaked one-mip. I am *not* a Lilliputian. I *am* Metaphor – or at least, my avatar inside the Web today. This is *me*. I can't spin out, and I'm in *trouble*. Now, are you going to help me, or not?'

I could see comprehension growing on his big, moon-like face. It was a classic double-take. 'You're serious, aren't you?'

I kicked my legs and waved my arms. '*Yes, I'm serious!*'

'Oh, wow.' He looked around. 'Come on. Let's go over to those tables and talk.' He started striding back towards the crèche.

I waved my arms. 'Wait.'

'What now?'

'You nearly stepped on my little brother.'

*

I was back on a tabletop again!

Surfer lifted the three of us up on to a padded tablecloth. He sat down and rested his huge head on his folded arms, studying us. I told him the whole story as quickly as I could.

'. . . and so we can't spin out. Not until we get inside the palace and grow back to normal size.'

'Then we've got to get you inside the palace,' he said. He frowned. 'I wonder who's behind all this? I wonder who the Empress really is?'

I turned to Clefven who was sitting squat-legged nearby. He looked back at me sternly, and would not reply.

There are a *lot* of villains in the Web. It is surprising what you can get up to if you're determined: fraud, theft, stalking people, interfering with programs, hacking into home systems – even destroying them.

There are also more subtle dangers, once you're inside the Web yourself: various creepy groups who try to subvert your mind with sleeper memory patterns called engrams. If you have an engram in your head, one day you wake up to find you've become a religious nut, or a flying-saucer fanatic, or you're eating your kid brother for breakfast . . .

Not that *that* would be so terrible.

There are police, called Webcops. The Webcops are an offshoot of Interpol who keep an eye on the crooks in the Web. But the Web is big, the crooks are smart, and the technology changes all the time . . .

It's a dangerous place, the Web. But then so is Realworld.

Surfer stood up and looked at the Imperial Court walls beyond the moat. 'Maybe I can get you in there.'

Clefven said, 'No. You'd never get across the moat. And even if you did, visitors aren't allowed in the palace.'

Surfer laughed. 'Visitors aren't allowed to do a lot of things.'

'Believe me,' Clefven said heavily, 'you won't make it.

They'll hurt you. Golbasta and her familiars . . . *We* can get inside if we can get across the moat, but it's pointless you even trying.'

Surfer laughed again. 'Uh – *hel-lo-oh*. Reality check here. This is the Web, remember? Nobody can get hurt in here. It's designed that way.'

'Haven't you been listening?' If I'd been big enough I would have punched him. As it was I had to make do with a lecture, brief and to the point.

After that, he was a bit less cocky. 'Then what can we do?'

'The most useful thing you can do is go to a data-box and send a message out,' I said. 'Talk to my dad.' I gave him Philip's name and his code. 'Tell him what's happening here. He'll have to come home from work and get us out.'

'I'll do it.' He frowned. 'But it might take some time.'

I sighed. 'I know.' I glanced at Byte who was playing with giant blobs of slime. 'By then, it might be too late. We have to go on.'

Clefven nodded. 'It is still up to you to save yourself, Metaphor. But we have a big problem.'

'What?'

'The moat around the Imperial Court,' he said. 'The drawbridge is up, of course. And without it we have no way across.'

Surfer grinned. 'It so happens I have an idea about that. Maybe there's another way I can help you.'

CHAPTER THIRTEEN

MOAT

Surfer hunted quickly around the crèche, collecting up some stuff. Then he picked up the three of us, lodged us in a pocket of his jacket and strode off out of the crèche and across the paved surround of the moat.

It was quite comfortable up there with my arms hooked over the lip of the pocket. I could look down and see Surfer's legs working like gigantic articulated machinery. Every step he took we bounced up and down in the pocket. I never realized before what a violent action walking is.

Byte was having fun. Maybe he thought this was another ride, the 'Giant-American-Kid' adventure. He was dangling his arms over the pocket and kicking.

The second time he kicked *me* he got kicked back.

We reached the edge of the moat. Surfer lifted us out one by one and placed us down on the paving stones.

To give him credit, he was a lot more careful than he had been before. But I still ended up rolling out of his hands and tumbling across the ground. Being ten centimetres high is just *not* dignified.

I got up and faced the moat. It looked as wide as the Thames. The surface was featureless except for a couple of lily pads – gigantic, bigger than the monsters I once saw in the hot-house in Kew Gardens.

One of the lily pads was rippling, I noticed, bobbing up and down as if something had just jumped off it into the water. But I couldn't see anything. I put it out of my mind.

Big mistake!

'Wow,' Byte said. 'It looks scary. I wonder if there are sharks in there.'

I said, 'Right now, a goldfish would be big enough to nip your head off.'

'There are no fish in GulliverZone,' Clefven said. 'One feature they haven't got around to yet.'

'So what now? Do we swim across?'

Surfer grinned. 'I have a cunning plan. You need a boat, right?'

'Yes. So?'

He reached down and pulled that inflatable baby's plastic boat out of his pocket. 'Welcome aboard the USS *One-Mip*!'

We inspected the toy. It was a piece of vacuum-formed plastic, as fragile in this world as the real thing would be outside. To us, it looked about the size of a small car.

'You have *got* to be kidding.'

'No. I've got it all figured out. That thing will float. And look at this.'

He dug into his pockets and pulled out a plastic tea-set spoon. It was about half my height, and easy to pick up.

Clefven laughed. 'I get it. Paddles.'

Byte, of course, thought it was terrific. It was just the kind of dumb toy he makes for himself at home anyhow. He started clambering all over the boat, making pirate noises. His grin was wider than the one painted on the plastic sailor glued inside the toy.

'I've never seen anything so ridiculous in my life,' I said. 'It's a *toy*, for heaven's sake.'

Surfer looked a little hurt. 'If you have a better idea, I'd like to hear it.'

Clefven picked up a spoon. 'I think you're being un-charitable, Metaphor. It's a masterpiece of improvization. I think your friend's done well.'

'Thank *you*,' said Surfer.

I sighed. Going to sea in a toy was the worst idea in the world. Except for staying here and doing nothing at all.

I had a feeling of deep and dark foreboding, but I tried to put it aside. The waters were calm and empty, after all. As long as the stupid boat floated, what could go wrong?

What, indeed!

Surfer lowered the boat into the water. Then he lifted us into it one by one, and passed us our spoons. With that big plastic sail sticking up – not to mention the big dumb toy sailor we had to share the boat with – the toy wasn't too stable. It rocked back and forth on the gentle swell of the moat.

Byte was running around being a pirate. If I'd had a plank I'd have made him walk it, there and then.

Surfer lay down on the ground so his huge head was facing us. 'There's no breeze,' he said. 'I'll blow you over as far as I can. But after a couple of metres you're going to have to use the paddles.'

Clefven waved. 'Thanks for all your help.'

'I'll tell your dad, Metaphor,' Surfer said. 'Don't worry. We'll get you out of this.'

I nodded, and clutched my spoon.

Surfer took a deep breath and blew out, hard and long.

Our 'sail' billowed with a plastic crackle. We set off with a lurch that sent Byte tumbling backwards.

Surfer stood up, waved, and ran off so as not to attract attention from the struldbrugs. He looked like a mobile mountain as he disappeared.

We came to rest. The shore already looked an awfully long way away. The water heaved slowly beneath us, its thick and oily surface catching the sunlight.

I longed to be out of there, back in my normal life, not bobbing about like a fragile little doll in this ridiculous toy boat. But that wasn't an option.

We picked up our spoons and lifted their bowls over the side. I pulled my spoon's handle backwards. It was like paddling a pleasure-boat across a lake in some Realworld park, except the water was thicker and a little sticky.

Slowly, slowly, we began to move forward, towards the imposing walls of the Imperial Court. Byte couldn't help much – he was too little to reach the water effectively – and it was up to me and Clefven to do all the work. Pretty soon my shoulders and back were aching.

But we picked up speed, and as long as we didn't stop paddling we advanced rapidly towards the far shore.

For once I thought everything was going to work out for us.

And then – just ahead of the boat – two gigantic deformed eyes loomed out of the water!

Byte screamed.

Clefven shouted a warning. We tried to slow the boat down, but it was too late.

We collided with something soft and fleshy.

The eyes rose up further, staring in at us, and then a huge mouth, half as wide as the boat itself, came leering over the bow of the boat. The skin around the mouth was slimy and mottled by warts. Two huge paws came slapping on to the top of the boat, great long fingers covered in warty skin. And now a huge white throat and belly came lurching up out of the water. The boat tipped forward!

I nearly lost my paddle. Clefven had to hang on to the mast to save being thrown straight out into the water. Byte wailing, went tumbling down inside the boat once more.

That huge white throat pulsed. '*RIB-IT.*'

I recognized the noise.

'It's a frog!' I shouted to Clefven.

He looked irritated. 'Of course it's a frog.'

Byte came crawling out. 'I thought you said there were no fish here,' he accused Clefven.

'A frog isn't a fish. It's an amphibian. This is advanced programming you're seeing here. The frogs are part of the defence. And furthermore—'

'And furthermore, that amphibian of yours thinks this boat is a lily pad!' I shouted.

Those big front paws came slapping their way a little further over the plastic of the boat, like a diver's webbed feet. The boat tipped forward further, rocking.

I had time to say, 'I think—'

And then, with a huge lurch, the frog hauled its body out of the water and on to the boat. I caught a glimpse of two gigantic, muscly back legs, scrabbling at the boat's surface. Then our mast broke in half and crashed down over us, and the frog came sliding over the back of the boat.

The frog's big slimy belly came brushing over me, and then he twisted around, sliming me some more. Soon my face, hair and clothes were covered with gooey, stinking, translucent green glop.

And then, it scarcely seemed possible – things got worse.

The frog was too heavy. Our unstable boat started tipping over.

I was falling towards the black, oily water!

CHAPTER FOURTEEN

WALL

Is it possible to drown in a Websuit?

It was an experiment I didn't want to try!

The water didn't feel like water. It felt sticky and thick, like warm honey. And it got very dark, very quickly, as I fell deeper in.

I'm usually a good swimmer, but not in syrup.

I could see light above me. I faced that way and kicked my legs. I tried to keep my mouth shut. I hated to think what would happen if that sticky stuff forced its way into my mouth, Websuit or not.

I broke through the surface, and I bobbed like a cork, treading water. The surface around my chest was tight and clinging, almost painful. The surface tension of that liquid was strong to someone of my size. Next time you see a pond, take a look at the insects walking around *on* the surface and you'll know what I mean.

Our toy boat was upside-down, the straw mast floating forlornly beside it. The frog, evidently scared, had disappeared. I couldn't see Clefven. But there, I saw with relief, was Byte. He was clinging to one of the plastic spoons, with his hair matted down over his face.

I swam over to him through the thick, soupy water. I got hold of the spoon handle next to him.

'Are you OK?'

He gave me a glare that wasn't a bad impression of

Philip's don't-ask-such-stupid-questions look.

I pointed. 'We aren't far from the walls . . .'

'Where's Clefven?'

'I don't know.' Actually I was worried about him. Clefven lived here, in GulliverZone. His body was designed for this world. Maybe we couldn't drown. But *he* probably could.

I didn't want to say any of this to Byte.

'Come on now, let's kick . . .'

We leaned forward, holding the spoon side by side, and kicked at the water. It frothed behind us, and our feet glopped as they entered and left the surface.

It only took a couple of minutes before my toes were brushing on a sloping, stony bank. I stood up straight, held Byte's hand, and we walked the rest of the way.

Once we were out of the water we shook ourselves dry, like a couple of dogs. We were standing on a steep, rocky beach. A few paces away the walls of the Imperial Court rose up like a brick cliff, grey and forbidding.

And a little way along the beach, Clefven was lying on his belly, gasping.

Byte saw him and ran. 'Clefven! Clefven!'

When I got to Clefven I helped him lie on his side, and cradled his head in my lap. He was coughing, but he seemed to be recovering quickly.

'Are you all right?'

'Yes,' he said. 'I think so. I got stuck underneath the boat, and I got a crack on the head. When I came to, my lungs were full of water.' He sat up, brushed back his soaking hair and checked his sword was still in its pouch at his waist. 'Come on,' he said. 'We mustn't rest. It's not safe here. And we have a way to go yet.' He stood up, panting hard.

'You didn't say anything about frogs in the moat,' I accused him.

He looked at me. 'Would it have made a difference? We had to get across there anyway. If we'd been lucky—'

'In future,' I said, 'tell me.' I meant it. I hate giant frogs. But I was discovering I hated surprises more!

He nodded.

I looked around. 'We still have to get past this wall.'

'There is a way in,' he said. 'But it's a little—'

'Dangerous?' Byte asked.

Clefven looked at him grimly.

'Well, there's a change,' I said.

'Follow me,' Clefven said. And he began to walk steathily along the deserted, stony beach.

Byte and I followed in the forbidding shadow of the wall. After a while, I felt Byte's hand slip into mine.

After a few minutes we came to what looked like an archway cut into the wall. It was a little taller than me, so Clefven was going to have to stoop. It looked as if it was roughly cut into the wall – not finished properly – and it led into some kind of tunnel.

There were no lights inside. The tunnel snaked off into the darkness, invisible beyond a few paces.

'Yuck,' said Byte, and for once I had to agree.

'Come on,' said Clefven. He hoisted his sword, and stepped into the archway. 'Follow me. Don't lag behind . . .'

Soon, all I could see was his back, disappearing from the daylight.

It looked as if we didn't have a choice.

It pushed Byte ahead of me. 'It'll be OK.'

'Really?'

'Sure,' I lied. 'The wall can't be all that thick . . .'

He trotted in trustingly after Clefven. I followed.

Soon I was in pitch darkness.

I could hear Clefven and Byte, a little way ahead of me, but I could see nothing. I bumped into the wall a couple of times – try walking in a straight line in the dark! – and then, to guide myself, I held out a hand and ran it along the surface of the wall.

It felt as if something had just carved out that tunnel, very crudely. I could feel big grooves and gouges. Strangely, they seemed familiar.

We used to have a hamster . . .

The marks in the wall had been made by teeth.

Suddenly, two giant yellow eyes loomed out of the darkness!

I yelled and stumbled back against the lumpy tunnel wall.

I heard a high-pitched squeal. It was like feedback from huge amplifiers, deafening, almost painful. Those big yellow eyes flickered. For an instant, there was a hot breath on my face and the giant eyes were right in front of me, like car headlamps.

I held my hands up in the dark.

There was a wall of fur in front of me, thick, coarse, wiry. It seemed to go on forever.

And then it was gone. I heard a pattering of huge, soft paws on the ground, heading back the way we had come.

There was a hand on my shoulder!

I jumped into the air.

'Calm down. It's me, Clefven. Are you all right?'

I tried to get my breath. 'Yes. Yes, I think so. What was *that*?'

'Later. Let's get out of here.'

He turned, and led us deeper into the darkness.

It only took a few more minutes before I saw the end of the tunnel as a small disc of light, far ahead. The light got brighter, until at last we came stumbling into daylight.

We crouched in the mouth of the tunnel while

Clefven peered out. Byte looked scared again, but I tried to smile to reassure him I was OK.

'Clefven, what was that? Was it whatever built these tunnels?'

Clefven wouldn't meet my eyes. 'I don't want to discuss it.'

'You have to,' Byte said. 'My dad says it's better for us to know dangers. That's so we can cope with them.'

'It isn't that,' said Clefven.

'Then what?' I asked.

Reluctantly, he turned to me. 'I told you my people are descended from computer viruses. Originally viruses were mindless and destructive – that was the way the people who made them wanted them to be – but slowly we evolved intelligence. Communication. An ability to build, not just destroy, and to care for each other.'

'Yes. So?'

'So, not every family of virus made it that way. Some of them stayed mean.

'They got bigger, and more powerful, and more destructive . . . *They're still here*. They live like us behind the skirting boards of the Web, but all they do is destroy. The Webcops call them cyberats.'

'Oh.' Now I understood. 'And that's what I saw in the tunnel.'

'That's what made the tunnel. Cyberats are like the original viruses. It's what everyone thinks *we* are.'

'But why are you so upset?'

He looked me in the eyes. 'I'm ashamed.'

'Ashamed?'

'That thing in the tunnel wasn't just some monster. *It was my cousin*. Now do you understand?'

CHAPTER FIFTEEN

PALACE

Inside the Imperial Court, to my relief, everything was Lilliputian-sized. *Me*-sized.

There were clusters of grand-looking buildings, two or three stories high – I suppose two metres tall, on Surfer's scale. For us it was a little like being in the grounds of the Tower of London. People were moving between the buildings. Some of them were dressed in bright uniforms, like beefeaters. There were more barriers to cross before we got to the centre – walls and fences – but I could see there were big metal gates in the walls, all flung open.

And there, within the walls, at the heart of the compound, was the glittering face of the palace itself.

I stood up, newly determined. I'd come this far. Nothing was going to stop me now.

I took Byte's hand. 'Come on,' I said. And I strode out of the tunnel, towards the first of the gates.

Clefven grabbed my arm and pulled me back.

A pair of struldbrugs – reduced to our scale – came clumping past, moving between the buildings and around the walls and gates. They were evidently on patrol. The people avoided them, but didn't seem afraid.

Clefven pointed upwards.

Another struldbrug – giant-sized this time – was patrolling the top of the Court wall. Its eyes, on long stalks, were peering down into the Court itself.

'Nothing's ever easy,' I grumbled.

'This is Golbasta's citadel,' whispered Clefven. 'You have to remember that Golbasta has dust of both varieties. She can shrink you or grow you. Her struldbrugs can be whatever size she chooses.'

I asked, 'What about all the little people here? Why don't we ask them for help?'

Clefven said, 'I wish we could. But the "people" here aren't Lilliputians any more. Not like me and my family. They are just empty shells without souls. They won't help us, I'm afraid.'

'What happened to them?'

His only reply was, 'We're on our own here.'

He looked around, and tapped me on the shoulder. 'Come on. I think I know a way.'

Crouching down, keeping an eye out for struldbrugs, we followed Clefven to the nearest building.

It was a small, one-story construction, crudely assembled from big chunky bricks.

Clefven peered in through the door. 'It's safe.'

We crept inside.

'Oh,' Byte said. 'It's a *stable*.'

He was right. The building was lined with stalls, each containing a horse. There was straw scattered on the roughly-finished floor. On the walls, garish red and white uniforms were hanging.

Clefven went up to a stall. 'This is where the Empress keeps her Imperial Coach.' He rubbed the nose of a horse, a beautiful white mare with a long flowing mane, and she rubbed her face against his hand gratefully. 'Beautiful creatures, aren't they? Phaces, of course. But just like the real thing. So I'm told.'

'Expensive, I should think.'

He shrugged. 'Yes. But the Empress isn't just powerful in here, inside the Web. She has a lot of influence in

Realworld. She was actually one of the people who originally designed the Web, and made a lot of money that way . . .'

I felt a prickling of unease. That was similar to the legends we used to scare each other with. Legends of the Sorceress.

Byte whooped. 'Metaphor! Come and look at this! You won't believe it.'

I went to see.

He had found the Empress's carriage itself, at the back of the stable.

It was a giant Tennessee Fried Ostrich takeaway carton!

The 'coach' was just a big garish cardboard box in red and white, with a picture of a grinning ostrich on the top. It was as big – on our scale – as a large car. Holes had been cut in the lid to serve as seats, and in the corners four big round chocolate-digestive biscuits had been nailed, as wheels.

There were reins leading from the front of the box, bright red. Byte was *chewing* one of the reins. 'I think this is liquorice rope,' he said. 'But I can't taste a thing.'

Clefven laughed. 'Don't chew through the reins. We need them. It's all sponsorship, of course. Money talks, even to an Empress. And the children visitors do love to see the Empress riding around in a coach that looks as if you could make it out of a food carton. Makes them think they could make one themselves, you see.'

'Don't tell me,' I said. 'We are going to have to ride in *that*.'

'It's good cover for us,' he said. 'Anyway, the coach isn't the worst of it.'

'There's *worse*?'

He was holding up a uniform for me to put on.

It was an ostrich suit.

*

Soon my legs were coated in baggy yellow tights that ended in splayed brown feet. Bright red-and-white feathers were stuck to my backside. I was looking out of the ostrich's big gaping mouth. TENNESSEE FRIED OSTRICH was written up and down my scrawny neck.

It was not my proudest moment. I was *so* embarrassed, and *so* glad nobody from school was there to see me.

Byte looked, if anything, even more comical. His suit was too big for him, and his tights were wrinkled up under his knees. Nevertheless, he laughed at me as loud as he could.

I tried to look as threatening as my ostrich outfit would allow. 'If you *ever* tell anyone about this I will sell you to the Tennessee Fried Ostrich people *myself*.'

'Pack it in, you two,' Clefven grumbled. He had got the friendly white horse out of its stall and was leading it to the coach.

We backed the horse into the coach's cardboard traces, and harnessed it with the liquorice reins. Clefven jumped up to the driver's seat at the front, and Byte and I scrambled into the seats cut out of the lid at the back.

Clefven picked up the reins. 'Everyone ready?'

I tried to fix my feathery tail under me. 'As ready as we'll ever be.'

'To the palace!' He flicked the reins, and snickered encouragingly to the horse.

The horse's hoofs clopped on the stone floor as we set off with a lurch.

We emerged into the open air and crossed the courtyard.

I hadn't noticed before that this area was cobbled, with great big shining stones. I noticed now. The cardboard coach bounced up and down, rattling me in my seat, and the feathers of my suit got up my nose, making me sneeze.

Byte thought it was great fun. He laughed all the way.

He's such an embarrassment.

I thought everyone would stare at us – *I* would if I saw a takeaway ostrich carton the size of a car bouncing towards me – but nobody here, neither the people nor the patrolling struldbrugs, took any notice.

We passed through one gate without being challenged. Then we reached the wall around the palace itself. The last barrier.

A soldier with a long, mean-looking pike was standing at the open gate. 'You have the password?'

Clefven hesitated.

I frowned. The 'password' must be some Webware access code. Of course, we had no idea what the password was. But every security measure can be overridden. Especially when someone as self-centred and powerful as this Empress was involved.

The guard stepped forward menacingly, raising his pike.

I leaned forward, and said as imperiously as I could, 'Is there some problem, driver?'

Clefven understood what I was trying to do. He turned and winked. 'I'm afraid there is, ma'am.'

'Override the entrance protocol,' I told the guard. 'Drive on.'

The guard hesitated. 'But—'

'I said, *override*. Do you want the Empress to know *you* held up the delivery of her coach?'

I knew he had no soul, of course, so the guard couldn't be afraid. But no program is designed to *want* to be shut down and dumped out of computer memory.

'Proceed,' he said pompously – as if it was all *his* idea – and he stepped out of the way.

The coach rattled through the gate.

And there ahead of us sat the palace, as wide and grand and gorgeous as a giant's wedding cake.

There was a soft clatter behind me, and the coach tipped back. I heard a scraping, of chitin over cardboard.

'We've been expecting you,' came a snake-like, slithery voice. 'Why didn't you say you wanted to come to the palace? I'd have been delighted to bring you here personally . . .'

I turned.

A struldbrug, on our scale, had climbed up on to the coach. It was already holding a scared-looking Byte in its arms.

It had a human face, half-swamped by chitin. It was Reldresal.

CHAPTER SIXTEEN

EMPRESS

We were stripped out of our ostrich suits, and dragged by three struldbrugs into the palace. I caught glimpses of magnificent, richly-furnished apartments – one hall was lined with mirrors, sparkling with light – but the place was joyless. It was deserted, save for clattering, patrolling struldbrugs.

The struldbrugs, led by Reldresal, dragged us further and further into the heart of the palace. And the further we went, the darker it got. The only lighting was from tiny flickering candles. It was almost as if, here at the centre of the Empress's spider-web, nobody was bothering to keep up the fairy-tale illusion.

At last we came to a gigantic open space.

It was as if the core had been bombed out of the middle of a grand hotel. We were about a third of the way up one wall. The walls were lined with balconies, and I could see corridors leading off to the Lilliputian rooms on all the levels of the palace.

It was dark here, the only light coming from the tiny candles in the rooms and corridors lining the central chamber.

And there was something here, in the middle of the hollowed-out palace. Something huge and dark.

The struldbrugs prodded us forward. For a moment I feared they were going to throw us over the edge, but then

I saw there was a platform here, like a bird-table. It sat on an immense pillar which stretched to the floor of the central chamber. The struldbrugs pushed and shoved until we were all three of us on the platform.

I struggled, but Clefven stopped me.

'There's nothing we can do,' he said. 'They've taken our weapons.' He sounded defeated, without hope.

'He's right,' cackled Reldresal. That chitin-pocked face creased up in a caricature of a smile. 'You've lost, human.'

I looked into her ghastly insect eyes. 'No,' I said evenly. '*You've* lost. Whatever she promised you for this isn't worth it. You're the one who deserves pity, Reldresal.'

She reared up above our platform, and I thought she was going to kill me there and then.

But I stood my ground.

She backed off.

Somehow, despite our peril, I wasn't afraid of her any more. I'd told the truth. I did pity her.

The platform slid away from the wall.

It started with a jolt and we all fell over. The surface was slick, like a plastic tabletop, and I had trouble holding on. Byte was on all-fours, and he looked as if he wanted to cry. But he was resisting it. 'I'm OK,' he said.

He is a game little kid sometimes.

I crept to the edge. There was no rail or barrier. This platform was *not* designed with our safety in mind. The pillar it was mounted on must have been five metres tall – fifty times my height! The base was far beneath me and lost in the dark.

The platform stopped moving just as suddenly.

A huge voice boomed over us. '"Whatever she promised you for this isn't worth it," you said, child. Perhaps you're right. But how do you know, *until I offer it to you too?*'

We were poised near the top of that huge, amorphous

statue-shape. The voice seemed to be coming from some-where within.

Two eyes, each as big as a car windscreen, snapped open. They were *glowing*, bright red.

By their crimson light I could see the eyes were set in a huge face, sculpted of some hard, dark green substance. And that formless shape below was a giant body, a mound of inert flesh, under thick flowing cloth.

It was the Empress Golbasta, sitting like a spider at the heart of her Lilliput-spanning web. I was face to face with her at last!

Byte was crying openly now. Clefven was holding him, trying to soothe him.

I walked to the edge of our platform. I was poised right before those giant devil's eyes. 'What are you?' I de-manded. 'Are you human?' My voice must have been a gnat's squeak to her. My legs were trembling. But I tried not to let my fear show.

There was a rumbling, deep within that mountainous body. It might have been laughter. 'Only as long as I have to be. Only as long as something *better* isn't available.'

She shifted, and a monstrous, fleshy hand rose up before me. On one finger she was wearing a ring, a big gold band the size of a rain-barrel, set with a red ruby.

There was movement, far below, at the base of the Empress's pit. Green eyes. It was the black cat we'd encountered earlier, walking around the Empress's tree-trunk legs, its back arched. It looked up at me, hissing and spitting.

I shivered. So Clefven had been right; the cat was a creature of the Empress. I wondered uneasily what it had once been; was there some poor cat out there in Realworld, locked in a Websuit? Or was this, too, some lost human being?

At any rate it clearly *had* been dangerous . . . and we'd come within a few metres of it!

There were two Lilliputian cups on the Empress's giant palm. Those giant red eyes turned to regard the cups.

'Look,' she said. 'Here is what you have come so far to find. What a shame you can't have it. Dust. Simple dust. The red stuff makes you big, the blue stuff makes you small. And with it, I control the world.'

The red glow of her eyes faded. 'You must forgive me. I am still anchored to the world outside. I get so tired. So tired . . .' Those eyes brightened again and their light swept me like two searchlights. 'You have spirit. Perhaps I should recruit you rather than destroy you. Listen to me, child. Wouldn't you like to *stay* here?'

I frowned. 'What do you mean?'

'Here, in the Web . . . Think about it. When you are in the Web you can take on any form you want. As easy as putting on a new set of clothes. You can *be* anything, anybody. Nothing grows old. Everything is perfect, for ever . . . And yet every two or three hours *you* are dragged back out to that Realworld of pain and decay and age and death . . . *Wouldn't you like to live for ever*, here inside the Web?'

'That isn't possible. My real body will always be outside, at home, in a Websuit.'

'No,' she said, and her whisper was like wind through tall trees. 'It doesn't have to be so. *You can download.*'

I turned to Clefven. 'What's she talking about?'

He was still holding Byte. 'It's a new, experimental procedure. You can store your consciousness here inside the Web; your very soul, loaded in piece by piece. Your real body, outside, eventually withers away and dies. But you live on, in here.'

For one second, it sounded wonderful. *To be in the Web for ever;* to be whatever I wanted, to go wherever I liked, be whatever age I liked.

To live for ever!

So that was what Golbasta was offering. Who wouldn't be tempted by it?

But then I thought of Philip.

I thought of my friends at school. The memory of Mum. I even thought of Byte, the little egg.

It would be an awful thing, I thought, to let myself *die* – never to wake up again in my body, in my own bed.

'Well?' hissed the Empress. 'Have you decided? Are you *tempted*?'

'Don't listen to her,' snapped Clefven. 'It isn't what you think. And there is a terrible price to pay . . .'

I didn't need him to tell me that. I'd already decided.

I stood square in front of the Empress's gigantic, grotesque face. 'Yes, I've decided. I don't want what you're offering. I want to be myself. I want my life back.'

She opened her mouth. There were no teeth behind those black lips, and ropes of spittle laced that huge cavern like spider-webs. 'You sentimental little fool. Very well. If you are too stupid to accept my offer, I will turn to another who will.'

She swivelled her mountain of a head.

A gigantic door opened up in the far side of the chamber. Lilliputian rooms and corridors folded out of its way. From the darkness beyond the door, another giant figure walked in.

It was a girl, I saw. She was moving jerkily, and her face was so pale it seemed to float like a skull in the dim light of Golbasta's lair.

It was the Wire.

She bowed to the Empress. 'Yes, Majesty.'

The Empress raised her huge hand on which the two little cups of dust still stood. She pointed to us. 'It is your time, my child.'

The Wire turned to me.

I jumped up and down. 'Wire! Wire! It's me! Don't you recognize me?'

The Wire reached out a huge, trembling hand.

She was reaching for Byte!

I ran forward, knocked him aside, and threw myself into the Wire's fingers.

She closed a fist around my midriff, trapping my arms to my sides.

Once again I was lifted into the air.

She held me before her face. Her huge eyes were glassy and unfocused. I kept shouting at her, but she didn't seem to respond or even recognize me.

And then she opened her mouth and put my head inside!

CHAPTER SEVENTEEN

WIRE

Just as I felt her teeth closing under my throat, I heard Byte jumping up and down on the bird-table. 'Hey! Stop it! Put my sister down!'

For some reason, it distracted the Wire. Maybe she was reminded of home.

She pulled my head out of her mouth. Her face was a huge sheet of flesh in front of me, like a giant close-up on a cinema screen. She looked around, confused.

'Do it,' hissed the Empress. '*Eat her*.'

Still the Wire hesitated. Her fist kept closing, in jerks, and the breath was squashed out of me.

Now Clefven was calling me. 'Metaphor, this is the way downloading works. Golbasta has to steal mips. Computer power. That's what she's trying to get the Wire to do now. *To suck the mips out of your Web body*. All that will be left will be a shell, like the people in the courtyard. You'll die, Metaphor.'

I struggled to speak. 'That's why Golbasta is hunting Lilliputians.'

'Yes. She must consume us to survive. But the Wire won't become immortal, like the Empress. Not in any human way.'

I understood it all now.

The struldbrugs.

Clefven said, 'The Wire will live for ever . . . but as a familiar, the slave of Golbasta. Like Reldresal. Tell her, Metaphor!'

But, looking up into the Wire's blank, unhappy face, I wasn't sure if it was going to be possible to tell her anything, ever again. She was obviously on supertime. She had been going too fast, too long. And I didn't know what else Golbasta might have used to infect her Websuit. Outside, the Wire must already be badly Websick. And she would have one major case of the slows when she got out.

When – *if* any of us got out of here!

She squeezed me again, her grip spasming.

I called her name, over and over again. Finally she tipped her huge head and looked down at me.

She opened her maw of a mouth and started moving me slowly in once more.

I struggled, but it was hopeless.

Desperately, I bent down and bit the edge of her hand as hard as I could. She started, and for a moment I thought she was going to drop me.

She looked down at me, her eyes a little clearer. 'Metaphor?' Her voice was squeaky and too fast. 'What are you doing here?'

'I'm about to be killed by you!'

She looked confused. 'No, it isn't like that. The Empress says I'll live for ever. And you will, as part of me.'

'She's lying to you. Oh, yes, you'll live for ever.' I got a hand free and pointed dramatically at Reldresal. 'You'll live like *that*. Is that what you want?'

She looked at what was – from her point of view – a small and shiny bug. For a moment doubt crossed her huge, cloudy face. But she said angrily, 'If that's what it takes, yes. I'm never going back out there, Metaphor. Out to Realworld. *Never.*'

Behind her, the Empress cackled like a huge witch.

'Wire – Meg – you can't mean that.'

She held me up and shook me so hard my teeth rattled. 'Oh, yes I can. What is there for me out there?'

I tried to think. 'Is it your parents splitting up? Is that it?'

'No. Yes. I don't know! Maybe their splitting up was my fault.'

I didn't know what to say.

'Get on with it,' the Empress hissed, stirring.

But still the Wire was hesitating. 'It's easy for you, Sarah.'

'What do you mean, easy?'

'You're clever. You're good-looking.'

'Me?'

'Compared to *me*,' she said miserably. 'Even Clefven said so. And you saw how the boy Surfer looked at you.'

She was wrong about that, of course – at least I thought she was – but it wasn't the time to argue!

The Wire said, 'You'll never understand what it's like to be me.'

Suddenly – in spite of everything, in spite of the danger I was in – I felt truly sorry for her.

'Maybe you're right,' I said. 'But you'll never know what it's like to be *me* – with only one parent, who's never home, and a kid brother to look after. People never understand each other. All we can do is put up with each other. Listen, Wire, I'll make you a deal.'

She looked at me suspiciously. 'What?'

'Maybe we can never be friends. Or maybe we can. Anyhow, when we get home, I'll try to put up with you.'

She sniffed. 'All right. And I'll put up with you.'

I laughed. 'And we'll both try to put up with my egg of a brother . . .'

The Empress roared now, and her huge bulk shifted like an exploding volcano. I suddenly remembered where we were. The Empress prodded the Wire with her open hand. '*Kill her!*'

Those two Lilliputian cups of dust still sat on Golbasta's stiff palm.

I hissed, 'Wire, the dust. *Give me the dust.*'

It seemed to happen in slow motion.

Golbasta tried to snatch back her hand. But the Wire, still on supertime, had the advantage of speed.

She snatched the two little cups from Golbasta's closing fist. Then she put me and the cups down on the bird-table platform.

Reldresal jumped across from the wall!

The struldbrug moved in a blur of speed. She grabbed both Clefven and Byte by the throat. And she was holding Byte right by the edge of the table.

I stepped forward, the cups in my hand.

'Any closer,' Reldresal hissed, 'and the kid goes over.' There was almost none of her human face left on that shell of chitin now – just a sketch of a malicious smile.

'I'm sorry,' Byte blubbered. His eyes were bugging as he scrabbled at her throat.

'You don't have to be sorry,' I said. 'She's not going to hurt you.'

'Oh, yes I am,' the struldbrug said. But she stumbled back when I moved forward, my only weapon the two cups of dust.

I tried to remember what Golbasta had said. *Red and blue*: one to grow, one to shrink. But which was which?

If I got it wrong, I could turn Reldresal into a giant we couldn't resist . . . and we would be trapped as Lilliputians for ever.

The red, I decided. The red shrinks people. That was what Golbasta said.

Wasn't it?

With a confidence I didn't feel, I said, 'Goodbye, Reldresal.'

I prepared to throw the red dust over her – but I thought I saw a flicker of hope in the chitinous mask of her face – and at the last moment I turned and threw the *blue*.

The dust sparkled over her like sky-blue snow. Reldresal wailed, a thin, human sound.

She let Byte and Clefven go. They fell to the tabletop like two sacks of water.

Reldresal started to shrink.

It was like a balloon deflating. I could hear that awful half-human wail getting higher and higher, until it vanished into insect buzzing.

There was a tiny flash of light, a wisp of smoke.

Reldresal was gone.

I thought I understood. 'She was already small. When she got a second dose of dust, the size control programs shrunk her past the point where her avatar could be sustained. She's gone.'

Clefven grabbed my arm, and Byte's, and pushed us together. 'Never mind her. She can't hurt you now. Use the dust. Get out of here.'

'What about you?'

'I'll be fine.'

'Oh, sure—'

'*Use the dust.*'

Of course, he was right.

I threw the red dust up in the air and held Byte close. The dust fell over us like confetti.

I started to grow immediately.

It was an even odder sensation than shrinking. Suddenly, the bird-table platform was too small for me – I almost sat on poor Clefven! – and I jumped off, pulling Byte with me. At first we were falling, but we expanded so quickly that our feet had grown down to the floor before we had time to fall.

Our growth slowed as we reached our full size.

The three of us – Byte, the Wire and me – were side by side in the Empress's chamber. Now we were large again the chamber didn't seem so imposing. After all, it was just a shabby hole cut in the middle of a toy palace.

Golbasta was still there, waving her fleshy arms and cursing us. But she didn't have anything left to threaten us with.

Even the cat had gone, I noticed. Even the cat had abandoned her.

I lifted up Byte's wrist. 'Scuttle,' I ordered him.

For the first time since the day he was born, he did as I told him.

He pressed the panic button, and his avatar broke up into a cloud of grainy cubes of light, swirling in the air like butterflies. In a moment, the cloud had shrunk down to a point of light which winked out.

He was gone, and safe.

The Wire grinned at me. Now I was normal size again, I could see how ill she looked.

'See you outside,' she said.

'Yes. Go.'

She pressed her scuttle button and disappeared.

I was the last.

I turned to the bird-table. Clefven was there, once more in his doll-like – compared to me – Lilliputian dimensions. I picked him up carefully and lifted him off the table to the mouth of a corridor in the wall.

'Will you be all right?'

'Yes.' He waved up at me. 'I have to find my family. Now you're safe, stay away from GulliverZone!' And he turned and ran off, into the depths of the palace.

'I'll be back,' I whispered after him.

I turned to Golbasta. She had subsided, wheezing and exhausted.

She didn't seem frightening any more. She was just a sad old woman who was scared of dying.

She dropped her head, and her red eyes winked to darkness. I pressed my scuttle button.

*

I was lying on my back in the spare bedroom. I pulled my Websuit mask off my face.

Philip was standing over me in his work clothes. He was glaring down at me. It was his worst look of all: *I-trusted-you.*

I sat up. Byte was struggling out of my ridiculous old ballerina-style Websuit. The Wire was still lying inert inside Philip's suit, struggling for breath.

Philip said, 'What kind of state is this to come home? Sarah, you were responsible. How could you let this happen?'

'Philip,' I said. 'Dad. Listen to me. *We have to go back.*'

CHAPTER EIGHTEEN

EAGLE

Well, you probably read the rest in your me-paper.

Philip trusted me. He's good at that. Although, he said, in this instance it was a long leap of faith.

He listened to what I had to say. He called the Webcops, and they listened to *him*.

GulliverZone was shut down immediately. The Webcops went in and they got everybody out.

They found everything: the little warren of living Lilliputians, the struldbrugs, the hollowed-out palace.

But the palace was empty. Of Golbasta and her most senior struldbrugs, there was no sign.

Byte was exhausted. Philip fed him, then put him to an early bed. The Wire was pretty ill from Websickness and all that Webtime. She was taken into hospital for observation. But the doctor said she would recover, and I said I'd come to visit as soon as I could.

I meant to keep my promise to her.

When it was all done, I was amazed to find it was *still* World Peace Day!

Philip asked me if I was hungry. He offered to get me some Tennessee Fried Ostrich as a treat!

I am *never* eating ostrich again.

He made me a quorn protein chili. And then we sat in the kitchen and looked at each other.

'It's still early,' I said.

'Young lady, you've had quite enough Webtime for one day.' But he was wearing his I-have-to-say-no-but-keep-trying-look.

'I still have thirty minutes before I hit three hours Web for the day,' I said. 'Besides, it's been *hours* since we all came out.'

He pulled his lip. 'Where do you want to go?'

I checked the time.

There was only one place to be right now; the biggest event of the day.

The launch of the Mars mission!

'It's very educational,' I said. 'And—'

'All right,' he said. 'But on one condition.'

'That you come in with me this time?'

'You bet your life.'

I scowled. I'd already had to bet my life at least three times today!

Anyway, that was how I ended up sitting on a wooden bench at Cape Canaveral, along with Noel Gallagher.

It was Philip, of course. He just won't edit his old avatar. It was *so* embarrassing.

There were billions of visitors at the launch. You were probably there.

They soaked Cape Canaveral with cameras and microphones and gave it its own Web building block, just for the day.

Cape Canaveral is in Florida. I was sitting facing east across a river, and the rocket pad was beyond a line of trees on the horizon. To my left was the biggest building I had ever seen, a black and white block so huge it might have been built by Brobdingnagian giants. It is called the Vehicle Assembly Building, and it's where they used to put together Moon rockets, four at a time. It has sliding doors a hundred metres high.

The launch pad is called Launch Complex 39-A, and it's where they launched those primeval missions to the moon, back in the 1960s. But today there was a small, slim spaceplane tipped up against a gantry like a little white paper dart. It was a Prometheus-class second generation space shuttle called *Eagle*.

The pad was five kilometres from me – or rather, from the camera I was seeing it through. It was so far away it would take ten seconds for the sound of the launch to reach me here.

There was quite a buzz of excitement among the crowd, and a lot of famous faces. A big countdown clock hovered in the sky. A commentator talked about how the astronauts would be digging into Mars's big underground reservoirs of water to see if any Martian life had survived the three-billion-year ice age there.

'Psst. *Psst.*'

The voice was tiny, and came from beneath my seat. It was as if an ant had spoken.

I glanced sideways. Noel Gallagher, also known as my father, hadn't noticed anything.

I bent forward and pretended to fiddle with my shoe.

There was a man standing there, in the shadow under my bench. He was wearing a leather waistcoat and carrying a bow and arrow.

He was ten centimetres tall. It was Clefven.

He was waving, indicating I should come behind the stand.

I stretched casually. 'Philip,' I said, 'I think I'll take a walk.'

'Only ten minutes to ignition,' he said. He even *sounded* like Noel Gallagher.

'I won't go far. I won't miss anything.'

He smiled, and for a moment I could see the real Philip. It was his I-know-I-can-trust-you look, despite those eyebrows. 'Take care.'

'I will.'

I hurried around the stand.

Clefven was with his family, Skyresh and the two children. Skyresh smiled, and Drunlo and Clustril jumped up and down with excitement when they saw me.

'What are you doing here? You aren't supposed to come outside GulliverZone.'

Clefven tapped the side of his nose. 'We used to be viruses, you know. We haven't forgotten *everything* . . . Anyway, we wanted to thank you.'

'Me? I was the one who got you into so much danger.'

He laughed. 'I seem to recall that was actually your little brother, and he couldn't help it. *You* were the one who convinced the Webcops to drive out Golbasta. And to take us Lilliputians seriously. Everything's going to be better now. We're going to be given our own building block on the Web, as many mips as we need, and protection from Golbasta. Or anybody else who tries to do what she did. We even have a lawyer arguing our case for human rights at the International Court in New York.'

'That's wonderful,' I said.

'Yes, it is. They even think they can help some of the struldbrugs. And it's all thanks to you.'

'Here.' Now Skyresh stepped forward shyly. She was holding up a Lilliputian book. It was the size of a thumbnail. She said, 'It's a gift. To say thank you.'

I leaned down and took the book. The paper was brown, the cover cracked. I turned the little pages with my fingertip. They were stiff and yellow-brown with age. *Travels Into Several Remote Nations of the World in Four Parts* . . . 'Oh,' I said. 'It's *Gulliver's Travels*.'

'The original and best. I hope you like it,' Clefven said. 'We put a full-sized edition on to your hard drive for you.'

'Thank you,' I said. 'I'll read it.'

(I did, later. And I had an eerie feeling of *déjà vu*. Gulliver had experiences like mine – but even *worse*. I wish I'd read the book before I went anywhere near GulliverZone!)

Clefven said, 'We have to go. But there's someone else who wants to see you.'

'Who? Where?'

He pointed to the Vehicle Assembly Building.

One of those huge sliding doors was opening.

When I stood at the base of the building, it was like looking up at a painted cliff face. I felt like a Lilliputian again.

And then a giant stepped out, eclipsing the bright Florida sun. I saw a smiling girl's face, bending down towards me like a hot-air balloon coming in to land.

It was Glumdalclitch.

'I'm glad to see you looking well,' she whispered in a voice like the wind.

'It wasn't so bad,' I said. 'We even enjoyed some of it.'

'We didn't catch Golbasta, you know.'

'Is that her real name?'

She shrugged, and shoulders the size of mountains heaved. 'It's the name of the avatar you met. Which she's now closed down. She has many avatars.'

The Sorceress, I thought with a shiver. Maybe those silly playground rumours held some truth . . .

But Glumdalclitch wouldn't say. She looked up at the artificial sky. For a moment she looked afraid, despite her huge size. 'She's still out there. I'm afraid that one day we are going to have to track her to her lair, and confront her.'

'"We"?'

'I'm a Webcop.' She smiled. 'I'm here to help. The one thing I don't understand is why you didn't just call for me when you got into trouble in GulliverZone. I said you could, right at the start. It's what I'm here for.'

I felt my jaw drop. 'Byte—'

'Who?'

'My kid brother. He kept saying we should call you. I didn't listen.'

Glumdalclitch laughed, and winked at me. 'I won't tell him if you don't.'

'Thanks,' I said with feeling.

'But if you're in trouble in the Web in future, don't forget to call.' She looked to the east. 'The launch is about to start.'

I turned. There was smoke billowing from the base of the spaceplane, and a voice was counting down: *five, four, three . . .*

Glumdalclitch was disappearing into the shadows of the Vehicle Assembly Building.

'I don't even know your real name!'

'Ariadne,' she said, her voice diminishing. 'Don't forget. *Call Ariadne . . .*'

There was a blue flash, and she was gone.

I looked over at Launch Complex 39-A.

A pure white light burst from the base of the *Eagle*, a splash of brilliance as bright as the Sun. The spaceplane rose suddenly, clearing its launch tower in a second. It rose up on a pillar of smoke, impossibly fast.

It all happened in eerie silence.

A spaceship was going to Mars! Everyone was clapping and cheering.

There was a sparkle of light next to me, cubes of colour that swarmed around each other like butterflies. They coalesced into a boy in a black gaming suit and a red cloak.

Surfer.

He grabbed my arm. 'Metaphor.'

'You missed the launch,' I said.

'What launch? Never mind that. *Listen! You won't believe what I found out about Dreamcastle . . .*'

The noise of the spaceplane reached me. The ground

shook and there was a sound like thunder in the sky, crackling and slapping. It was as if Brobdingnagian giants were walking by, laughing.

WEBSPEAK – A GLOSSARY

AI   Artificial intelligence. Computer programs that appear to show intelligent behaviour when you interact with them.

avatar or realoe   Personas in the Web that are representations of real people.

basement-level   Of the lowest level possible. Often used as an insult, as in 'You've got a basement-level grasp of the situation.'

bat   The moment of transition into the Web or between sites. You can 'do a bat' or 'go bat'. Its slang use has extended to the everyday world. 'bat' is used instead of 'come in', 'take a bat' is a dismissal. (From *Blue And Tone*.)

bite   To play a trick, or to get something over on someone.

bootstrap   Verb, to improve your situation by your own efforts.

bot   Programs with AI.

chasing the fade   Analysing what has happened in the Web after you have left it.

cocoon   A secret refuge. Also your bed or own room.

cog	Incredibly boring or dull. Initially specific to the UK and America this slang is now in use worldwide. (From *Common Or Garden* spider.)
curl up	'Go away, I don't like you!' (From *curl up and die*.)
cyberat	A Web construct, a descendent of computer viruses, that infests the Web programs.
cybercafe	A place where you can get drinks and snacks as well as renting time in the Web.
cyberspace	The visual representation of the communication system which links computers.
d-box	A data-box; an area of information which appears when people are in Virtual Reality (VR).
download	To enter the web without leaving a Realworld copy.
down the plug	A disaster, as in 'We were down the plug'.
egg	A younger sibling or annoying hanger-on. Even in the first sense this is always meant nastily.
eight	Good (a spider has eight legs).
flame	An insult or nasty remark.
fly	A choice morsel of information, a clue, a hint.
funnel	An unexpected problem or obstacle.
gag	Someone, or something, you don't like very much, who you consider to be stupid. (From *Glove And Glasses*.)
glove and glasses	Cheap but outdated system for experiencing Virtual Reality. The

glasses allow you to see VR, the gloves allow you to pick things up.

Id   Interactive display nodule.

mage   A magician.

mip   Measure of computer power

nick or alias   A nickname. For example, 'Metaphor' is the nickname of Sarah.

one-mip   Of limited worth or intelligence, as in 'a one-mip mind'.

phace   A person you meet in the Web who is not real; someone created by the software of a particular site or game.

phreak   Someone who is fanatical about virtual reality experiences in the Web.

protocol   The language one computer uses to talk to another.

raid   Any unscheduled intrusion into the Web; anything that forces someone to leave; a program crash.

realoe   See *avatar*.

Realworld   What it says; the world outside the Web. Sometimes used in a derogatory way.

scuttle   Leave the Web and return to the Realworld.

silky   Smarmy, over enthusiastic, untrustworthy.

six   Bad (an insect has six legs).

slows, the   The feeling that time has slowed down after experiencing the faster time of the Web.

spider   A web construct. Appearing in varying sizes and guises, these are used to pass on warnings or information

	in the Web. The word is also commonly applied to teachers or parents.
spidered-off	Warned away by a spider.
spin in	To enter the Web or a Website.
spin out	To leave the Web or a Website.
SFX	Special effects.
strand	A gap between rows of site sky-scrapers in Webtown. Used to describe any street or road or journey.
suck	To eat or drink.
supertime	Parts of the Web that run even faster than normal.
TFO	Tennessee Fried Ostrich.
venomous	Adjective; excellent; could be used in reference to piece of equipment (usually a Websuit) or piece of programming.
vets	Veterans of any game or site. Ultra-vets are the *crème de la crème* of these.
VR	Virtual Reality. The illusion of a three dimensional reality created by computer software.
warlock	A sorcerer; magician.
Web	The worldwide network of communication links, entertainment, educational and administrative sites that exists in cyberspace and is represented in Virtual Reality.
Web heads	People who are fanatical about surfing the Web. (See also phreaks.)
Web round	Verb; to contact other Web users via the Web.
Websuit	The all over body suit lined with receptors which when worn by Web

	users allows them to experience the full physical illusion of virtual reality.
Webware	Computer software used to create and/or maintain the Web.
widow	Adjective; excellent; the term comes from the Black Widow, a particularly poisonous spider.
wipeout	To be comprehensively beaten in a Web game or to come out worse in any Web situation.

OTHER TITLES IN
THE WEB SERIES

FEEL UP TO ANOTHER?

DREAMCASTLE by Stephen Bowkett

Dreamcastle is the premier fantasy role-playing site on the Web, and Surfer is one of the premier players. He's one of the few to fight his way past the 500th level, one of the few to take on the Stormdragon and win. But it isn't enough, Surfer has his eyes on the ultimate prize. He wants to be the best, to discover the dark secret at the core of Dreamcastle. And he's found the girl to take him there. She's called Xenia and she's special, frighteningly special.

He's so obsessed that he's blind to Rom's advice, to Kilroy's friendship and to the real danger that lies at the core of the Dreamcastle. A danger that could swallow him whole . . . for real.

DREAMCASTLE, it's no fantasy.

DREAMCASTLE ready for access June 1997.

THINK YOU'RE UP TO IT?

UNTOUCHABLE by Eric Brown

Life might be easier for most people in 2027 but for Ana Devi, whose only home is the streets of New Delhi, it's a battle for survival. She's certainly never dreamed of visiting the bright virtual worlds of the Web. And when her brother is kidnapped the Web is certainly the last thing she is thinking about. But the Web holds the secret to what has happened to her brother and to dozens of other New Delhi street children.

How can Ana possibly find enough money to access the Web when she can barely beg enough to eat each day? Who will help her when her caste means that no will even touch her? Somehow she must find a way or she will never see her brother again.

Dare you touch the truth of UNTOUCHABLE?

UNTOUCHABLE ready for access October 1997.

TAKE ANOTHER WALK ON THE WILD SIDE
SPIDERBITE by Graham Joyce

In 2027 a lot of schooltime is Webtime. Imagine entering Virtual Reality and creeping through the Labyrinth with the roars of the Minotaur echoing in your ears? Nowhere near as dull as the classroom. The sites are open to all, nothing is out of bounds. So why has Conrad been warned off the Labyrinth site? There shouldn't be any secrets in Edutainment.

Who is behind the savage spiders that swarm around Conrad whenever he tries to enter the site? And why do none of his friends see them? There is a dark lesson being taught at the centre of the Labyrinth . . .

SPIDERBITE, school was never meant to be this scary . . .

SPIDERBITE ready for access October 1997.

ARE YOU READY TO GO AGAIN?
LIGHTSTORM by Peter Hamilton

Ghostly lights out on the marsh have been the subject of tales and rumours for as long as anyone can remember but the reality is far more frightening than any ghost story. Something is going wrong at the nearby energy company and they are trying to keep it a secret. Somebody needs to be told. But Aynsley needs help to do it. The Web keeps him in touch with a network of friends across the world and it might just offer him a way in past the company security to find out exactly what's going on.

But the Web works both ways. If Aynsley can get to the company then the company can get to him. And the company has a way of dealing with intruders.

LIGHTSTORM, sometimes it's best to be in the dark.

LIGHTSTORM ready for access February 1998.

IS THIS THE END?

SORCERESS by Maggie Furey

A fierce and menacing intelligence is corrupting the very heart of the Web. Vital research data is being stolen. Someone or something is taking control of a spectacular new gamezone. The Web is no longer safe. The Sorceress continues to outwit all who attempt to destroy her, but her time is running out and she will stop at nothing to get what she wants. Someone must stop her.

Only one person has the power to overcome the awesome creator of the Web.

But who could survive a battle with the Sorceress?

SORCERESS ready for access February 1998.